**Did she really think she could get away from him on a train? Where would she hide?**

The compartment lock turned.

Key.

Not Jo. Not the steward.

He wanted to let whoever threatened inside, catch them, eliminate the danger.

He shot across the room as soundlessly as he could, pulled Jo down with him on the floor, covering her mouth as she woke. As best as his six plus feet could manage, he rolled on top of her to protect her from assault.

He recognized the momentary panic in her eyes that quickly subsided, shifting to question.

Shh. He mouthed the age-old sign to be quiet and braced for an attack.

The door had slid inches, but no one entered.

He lowered his mouth to her ear. "I'm going to move toward the berths and you're going into the shower."

She nodded and they repositioned. He quickly got to his back with his gun pointed toward the door.

Nothing.

"Could it have been someone who had the wrong compartment?" she whispered a minute later.

"Door was locked."

She stared at the three-inch opening. "What does this mean?"

"Whoever's trying to kill you…is on this train."

# ANGI MORGAN

## DANGEROUS MEMORIES

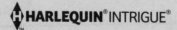

HARLEQUIN® INTRIGUE®

First to my "sprint" buds: Thank goodness for "the magic room."
I hope it doesn't appear silly for me to dedicate my story to a couple of dogs.
But over the past thirteen years, I've spent more time with my (first ever) pets
than human beings. Each reminded me to take a break and play. Each reminded
me about unconditional love. And each will be remembered in my heart forever.
Without Logan and Pepper, life wouldn't have been as rich, or nearly as funny.
They can never be replaced, only remembered with tremendous love.

ISBN-13: 978-0-373-69673-4

DANGEROUS MEMORIES

Copyright © 2013 by Angela Platt

Recycling programs
for this product may
not exist in your area.

Printed in U.S.A.

## ABOUT THE AUTHOR

Angi Morgan had several jobs before taking the opportunity to stay home with her children and develop the writing career she always wanted. Volunteer work led to a houseful of visiting kids and an extended family.

When the house is quiet, Angi plots ways to intrigue her readers with complex story lines. She throws her characters into situations they'll never overcome... until they find the one person who can help.

With their three children out of the house, Angi and her husband live in North Texas with only the four-legged "kids" to interrupt her writing. For up-to-date news or to send Angi a note, visit her website, www.angimorgan.com.

## Books by Angi Morgan

**HARLEQUIN INTRIGUE**

# CAST OF CHARACTERS

**Jolene Atkins, aka Emaline Frasier**—For as long as she can remember, she's longed for a "normal" life, one free from lies. As the memories of her mother's murder begin to resurface, she has two choices: don't remember and look over her shoulder the rest of her life; or remember, enter the WitSec program living a lie and looking over her shoulder the rest of her life. Is there a third option?

**U.S. Marshal Levi Cooper**—He's the "go to" guy in the Denver Division Witness Security Program. A classic workaholic, but the guy who always keeps his word. He made a promise to Jolene's dad—and will die before breaking his word.

**U.S. Marshal Sherry Peachtree**—Levi's supervisor in the Denver office.

**FBI Agent George Lanning**—An acquaintance who's worked with Levi in the Dallas office and who is prepared to help in the search for the murderer.

**Elaine Frasier**—A Dallas defense attorney who discovered something so horrific she chose to turn federal witness but was murdered along with two U.S. Marshals twenty years ago.

**Joseph Atkins, aka Robert Frasier**—Jolene's father. A Dallas landscaper who entered the WitSec program to protect his daughter. He was recently killed in a suspicious car accident after he began looking into his wife's case.

**The Client**—Represented by Elaine Frasier, they arranged for her brutal murder before she could hand over any evidence. Have they been lying in wait for the Frasiers to return?

# Chapter One

"Gun!"

U.S. Marshal Levi Cooper did a three-sixty search for the person shouting or confirmation of an actual gun. He couldn't see anything, but he couldn't take a chance with Jolene's life. He moved. "Everybody down!" The few people attending the funeral heard the warning and scattered away from the casket.

All except the target.

So he ran. Slipping and sliding downhill through the mud and sheets of pouring rain, he ran to save her life.

He watched Jolene Atkins continue to stand under the canopy erected by the funeral home. Next to her father's casket, still suspended on the lowering system, her shoulders shook as if she were crying.

She didn't take cover.

Levi hurdled a flower arrangement to get to her faster. He should have listened to himself earlier and never left her side. He heard the shot. Choices? Either hit the dirt or run like those in his peripheral vision. He leapt in a flying tackle to take Jolene down with him.

He'd pushed hard off the slippery grass, heavily landing on top of her. He turned as much as he could to take the brunt of the fall. Their bodies slid off the fake-grass rug, into the mud.

Wreath stands fell onto the casket.

Roses and other flowers fell on their heads.

Rain pelted them like ice shards.

Levi rolled on top of her, keeping his weight on his elbows and knees, using the bulletproof vest he wore to shield her heart. If it were only that easy.

"Are you all right?" he asked.

Jolene shook her short dark hair and wiped the rain from her face. Was the hitch in her breathing and wide-eyed confusion from falling or recognition he was there?

"You."

Recognition. She twisted trying to free herself. "I should have known you'd stoop to dramatics to prove yourself right."

"What's that supposed to mean?" He eased his body the opposite direction he wanted her to roll.

"I'm not going anywhere with you." She shoved him aside, and a bloodred carnation fell to the puddle between them. On her stomach, she put her hands in the mud and curled her toes.

He'd knocked her right out of her shoes.

"Did you have to ruin his funeral?"

"We need cover." Ignoring her accusations, he jerked her hand into his, forcing her close to his side. He pulled his weapon from its holster. Not a good situation. No backup. No idea who had pulled that trigger.

The shot had definitely come from the top of the hill behind them. On their knees, he awkwardly draped an arm over Jo, keeping her body low to the ground until they could sit with the coffin at their backs—the only cover he had.

"Did you stage this?" she asked, one hand in a fist, the other pointing toward the trees.

The coat she wore was thin and already soaked through. She'd be frozen in a matter of minutes.

"Stage a guy trying to kill you at your father's funeral?"

"I wouldn't put it past a devious person to do anything to get what he wants."

"I thought this site was a bad idea." He didn't blame her. He'd been against having the funeral in St. Louis from the start. She'd insisted on using the plot next to her mother's.

"Four years ago, you and my father assured me he was no longer in witness protection."

Yeah, she was angry. Someone had just taken a shot at her and she was yelling at *him*.

"One problem at a time. I can't see a shooter."

The trouble really began when Levi tried to explain why her father had convinced her he was no longer in the witness protection program. Explaining was difficult when he didn't understand why Joseph had lied, either.

"Jolene, I'm here against orders because I'm probably the only person left who believes your father." *Believed.* A week had passed and it was still hard to think of Joseph as dead. "Why won't you trust me?"

"You lied." She drew her knees up to her chin and hid her face. "You both lied."

Levi couldn't respond. It was a truth he couldn't deny or justify at the moment. Helping her would keep his promise to her dad but it wouldn't make her feel better. Wanting to comfort her was a part of attending the funeral. He knew how hard it was to say goodbye to a parent. Not exactly under these circumstances, but he knew. There wasn't any time for comfort.

The sound of car engines faded and the whine of police sirens grew.

Mourners were gone. Flower arrangements were destroyed. No sounds other than the tent canopy flapping

in the wind and rain pelting the tarp. The chance to say goodbye with dignity was done. Jolene couldn't hear his professionalism shattering within his mind.

"Is there any reason to continue sitting in the mud?" she asked, wiping rivulets of water from her face.

"Give me a minute to check things out." Making demands had never worked with Joseph Atkins's daughter. Hadn't worked with him, either.

She seemed to accept his statement, remaining still while he zigzagged from one headstone to the next, attempting to draw another attack. Nothing happened. No one in sight. Even the cemetery workers had fled.

"Let's go, Jolene." He raised his voice and ran back to the gravesite, swiping at his wet face. "We need to leave before the cops haul us in for questioning."

"Your big marshal badge won't keep the police at bay?" She pushed back her hair and seemed to notice the strewn disorder around them. "I can't leave things like this." She immediately set flowers straight, scooped her heels from where she'd originally stood and stuffed them in her coat pockets.

His badge wouldn't give him any authority over Jolene and he had no official reason to be in Missouri. Jolene stopped short at a small headstone—the one placed to declare her death and escape into WITSEC.

"Jo…" He took her elbow and gently tugged her toward his car. "He'd want you safe."

"But—"

"No buts. We're going."

They skirted the edge of the cemetery back to his rental car, exiting through the gate opposite where the police entered. Joseph Atkins would rest in peace next to the wife he'd never stopped loving. Which was the reason Levi had

finally agreed to bury him where friends thought he'd been buried for twenty years.

Five minutes down the road with the heater blasting on high, Jolene took a visible, deep breath. The tears seemed to be over for the moment. He needed her calm. Thinking straight.

"What are you doing here, Levi? Or should I call you Marshal Cooper?"

"I came to say goodbye to a good friend."

"Don't you mean client? Or witness? I can't believe Dad kept this from me. Why? What was the point? How could you have gone along with it?"

"I admit that being introduced to you as a family friend wasn't my idea, but your dad did what he thought was right. He was always thinking about your safety."

"Come on, Levi. Does this really seem like the *best* thing to you?"

They were both soaked to the skin, making him wish he'd rented a car with warming seats. Her makeup was circling her emerald eyes from both tears and the rain. Did it look like the best thing? Not by a long shot, but she was alive.

"In the past week, my father died in a car accident. The United States Marshals Service advised that burying him next to my mother may alert her murderers to my whereabouts, but because I wasn't officially in the WITSEC program they couldn't help me. And you show up yesterday with a letter supposedly from my father."

"It's real."

"Stow it. He lied for four years, he's lying now. I did not witness my mother's murder." She shook her short hair so hard drops of water sailed across the car. "I've seen the best therapists WITSEC had to offer. Everyone believes I'm *not* a witness—except you."

"And your father. And the person who tried to kill you a half hour ago."

"If you hadn't shouted 'gun' we would have finished his service. In all the rain, you probably saw a stick or something."

"I didn't shout gun." So who had shouted? Someone who wanted the crowd out of the way?

One warning. One shot. One attempt. And no one tailing them. Didn't make sense. If they were tailed, he'd pull into one of the restaurants with rear street exits he'd found yesterday. Easier to elude a following car than attempt to outrun them.

"And I know the difference between a stick and gun. Even in the rain."

"Yes, but *you* are a liar."

"That does it." He quickly switched lanes, pulling into an empty fast-food lot and headed toward the Dumpster.

Stomping on the brakes, the rental skidded to a stop. He had it under control, but Jolene still held onto the dashboard. It took her a minute before she relaxed into the seat.

The rain continued. Hail pinged the roof a couple of times or he would have stood outside. He shook off his coat in the cramped space, pulled at the straps holding the vest in place and yanked it over his head, tossing both into the backseat.

"Would you take me to my hotel on Paige near Highway 270? Aren't you worried they're following us?" She shook her hands in the air. "Whoever *they* are."

"Yes, as a matter of fact I am." He shifted in the seat and hooked his arm over the steering wheel. "But let's get one thing straight. I did not willingly lie to you. I respected your father's wishes. For some reason he wanted you away from him. He said it was important for you to have a life outside of witness protection after you gradu-

ated. So I helped with that by keeping the fact I was his WITSEC handler to myself. I have to protect others every day. It's part of my job. But I am *not* a liar."

She didn't respond. He put the car in gear, checking the mirror often, turning suddenly a couple of times without using his indicator. Just in case the gunman was following. He couldn't see much with the rain pelting the car. The back window was foggy, obscuring his ability to watch for cars that may have followed.

"My mother's murder was a long time ago, Levi. And I honestly don't remember anything about it. I was hiding. It's in every report. Hiding in my toy box."

Jolene's resolve was straightforward, confident. The same person he'd grown to admire during his visits with her father. Okay, he could admit that all the visits hadn't been just to see a man well settled in the life WITSEC had provided. Maybe a few of the visits had ulterior motives. Extra Sunday dinners or even Monday leftovers. Extra visits with both the Atkinses.

"The triple homicide involving your mother is an ongoing investigation. They never caught or identified all the men your father saw. The man he put away was killed shortly after arriving in prison." Time to be honest about everything. "One of the guns was used in three other murders as recently as six months ago."

"Why did he keep this from me?"

"I can't answer that, Jo. What I can do is get you back to WITSEC and to someone who will help you remember."

"I can't do that."

The confidence was gone. Even the idea of trying to remember seemed to frighten her.

"With the proper help—"

"Let me say it a different way. I *won't* remember. Why

would anyone try to remember their mother being slashed to death?"

"To stay alive."

The sincerity Jolene saw as Levi said the simple words scared her to her marrow. He meant it. And she believed him.

The words resonated, bouncing around in her head. *Stay alive.* An echo of something. But her father had said those words her entire life. Everything they'd done was in order to stay safe…to stay alive.

"You really think they want me dead? I was only five when it…when Mama…"

"Hey," he said with a comforting sigh. He watched the road, but his hand slid across hers, covering her shaking fingers, warming the chill away. "There's time to talk later. Right now we should pick up your suitcase and change into dry clothes."

So much, so fast. Too fast.

She removed her hand from under his, deliberately meshing her fingers together and tucking them under her chin. He was a U.S. Marshal. Not a confidant. Not her father's colleague. And never her true friend.

She may trust Levi Cooper with her life, but not any part of her heart.

Been there. Done that. Saved the hurt.

Waiting to discuss the details was fine. She was cold, wet, emotionally overwhelmed and at the moment, easily swept up into the idea of danger she'd been cautioned about her entire life. She didn't know if she believed Levi's gun sighting, but she wanted to see the letter her father had written.

Her father's precautions had kept her safe for twenty years. But she had no intention of traveling to wherever

the marshal wanted her to talk with more experts. Nothing would bring back the memories.

Nightmares were just nightmares.

Speeding through the first couple of yellow lights seemed normal. He was on edge and she'd been lost in thought. But when Levi gripped the wheel tighter, slowed for the yellow, then sped up through the red, she knew there was a problem.

"You could give a girl some warning." Her bare feet were pressing hard on the floorboard, trying to stop the car, then just keeping her in her seat.

"How did they find us? Nobody followed from the cemetery." He slammed his palm on the steering wheel.

"Honestly, if you think I'm going to fall for—"

She turned around to see a black car run the light, causing a chain reaction crash with crossing traffic that tried to avoid a collision. She verified her seat belt was tight and clenched the dash again. "I don't believe this is happening."

"Believe it."

Levi drove like a professional racer, darting in and out and around the cars in their way. Skidding around corners in the rain. The black car stayed right with them—never gaining, never falling behind.

"You can't keep driving like this. You aren't that lucky. They won't have to kill us because you will."

There was no difference in Levi's expression. No recognition that his thoughts may have gone to her father's death in a car accident. He seemed to concentrate on his driving too much to look at her, but she could stare nowhere else except at him. If she watched the cars or the road or paid too much attention to the close calls, she'd begin to panic. She couldn't control the helplessness building in her throat. It was buried deep inside somewhere and bubbled to the surface every time there was a near miss with a car.

"Why aren't the police following us yet?" she asked, keeping her focus on Levi's eyes. "Wouldn't that get these guys off our backs? Can I call them?"

"It might, but I think it's both good and bad. So let's skip the local explanations and go straight to the airport."

"Skip talking to the police and just leave town?"

He slowed to exit the highway they'd been traveling on for a short time. Jolene looked at the road in time to see a sign for Lambert-St. Louis International Airport. So all his turns had been deliberate, heading here. Nowhere near where her chosen hotel was located. He'd planned this and she hadn't noticed where he'd been going.

They passed through the airport entrance and the black car continued down the road. They weren't being followed any longer. They were safe.

For the moment.

"I didn't think they'd like the security cameras at the airport. I need you to use your phone and call the airline."

"You want me to leave now?" At first the cost of changing her ticket made her cringe, but at least she'd be sleeping in her own bed tonight. That thought made her sigh with relief. "My ticket to Atlanta is for tomorrow and all my stuff's at the hotel."

"Nothing that can't be replaced or shipped?"

"Fortunately, no." No makeup, no toothbrush. A trip to the store on the way home instead of straight to bed. Her bed. Was he coming with her? The thought tied her stomach in more knots.

He slowed the car to a crawl waiting for people crossing the street. He acted so calm and casual, leaning against the door, his hands relaxed on the steering wheel instead of his previous death grip. It was infuriating how he could turn the adrenaline on and off. Her heart was still beating

fifteen hundred miles an hour and her stomach was still ten miles back.

"My duffel's already in the trunk. Your hotel is too risky. These men know your name, where you live, what you do. I'm not sure how they found out, but it's a safe bet they've already tracked you through your phone."

"I'm not throwing away my phone." *Or giving up my life. Changing my name. Leaving everything behind. Or taking you home with me to my one bedroom apartment.*

"Who asked you to? We'll take out the battery."

"Oh."

Her heart had jump-started at his answer. What did he have planned? He parked in the first spot on the highest garage floor. No one was in sight. Just the rain beating a strange rhythm that made her nervous. Or being in close quarters with Levi did.

Or maybe it was the realization that someone believed she could recognize her mother's murderers and had attempted to kill her. Of course, that could have something to do with the urge to lose what little she'd had for lunch.

"If they're tracking my phone, why use it to change the tickets?" she asked. "We could just go inside."

He raised his eyebrows and grinned. With chocolate-colored wet hair curling on his forehead and dirt streaked across his dimpled cheek, he looked like a sweet, innocent little boy who had made his first mud pie.

"You *want* them to know about the ticket change?"

He nodded.

"Because we aren't going to use them."

"Right again. We're taking the train."

"Then how do I get back? Won't they just track me from wherever we're going?"

"We can't let that happen," he said flatly.

"Just so we're clear, I have no intention of returning to

Boulder." She'd already asked a college friend to oversee the sale of furniture and shipping of her father's things. "I can't talk to anyone about what I didn't see so it won't do any good to go back."

"You have to try. They were very clear that I can't take you into WITSEC until you're an actual witness."

"You're confusing me. Just tell me where we're going so I can say no."

"I was thinking about Dallas."

*No. No. A thousand times no.*

"But Dallas is where…"

"Where your mother was murdered."

## Chapter Two

"I'll never go back. Dad said *never* to go to Dallas or even Texas." Jolene's phone dropped to the floorboard.

Levi had assumed she wouldn't like his idea. He didn't like it, either. What he hadn't counted on was the absolute terror that reached the depths of her beautiful eyes. Just the thought of Dallas and she went somewhere far away.

"You did warn me 'no' would be your answer. Unfortunately, it's the only plan I've got." Partly his, partly her father's, but the only one.

She hadn't liked anything he'd said—today, yesterday or last week. When he'd made the official notification of her father's death, they'd had a moment. Minutes remembering someone they cared about, remembering how they'd met four years ago.

When he'd explained he was a U.S. Marshal and her dad had been under his watch, the moment was gone. She had four years of lies. That's all she could see and he didn't blame her. For him it was a relief to tell the truth. It would be a bigger relief to let her know he'd been keeping tabs on her, making certain she was safe while living in Georgia.

One thing at a time.

The current problem was how to change her mind so he could save her life. How could he get her to admit she was in serious danger? He couldn't jump over, dash around, or

break through the barricade she held in place. She hadn't spoken to him unless it concerned getting her dad's body to St. Louis. She acted like a person who couldn't accept her life was gone.

He understood that.

But this was different. She needed to listen to him.

Suppressing his natural tendency to issue an order took effort. He wasn't used to anyone doubting his advice, not to mention his word. And he wasn't used to those needing his help flat out rejecting his expertise.

"This is ridiculous," she said, seemingly bounced back from his announcement. "Right now, I'm not convinced there was a shooter, but if there was, how do you know the shooter was after me? It could be you he wants."

"I wasn't followed from Colorado and your mother's murderers didn't have a clue I knew your father." No sugarcoating. She needed to realize these men were out for her blood. He'd tell her about the second shooting later. "Say there wasn't a shooter. How do you explain the sedan following us?"

She shook her head, denying the obvious. "Why isn't it possible someone at your end sold out my dad?"

"Twenty years, Jolene. Twenty years of safety."

"Twenty years of safety just confirms there's not a problem."

"Based on your father's letter, I disagree. He told me you saw the murderers and if you remembered, you'd be in danger."

"See, that's your flaw. If there was any truth to the letter, I'd have *some* type of memory. Some clue that what you're claiming is true. And there's nothing. I've never remembered anything about that day. Ever."

Joseph's letter stated she'd had dreams that were becoming more frequent. Her reluctance to admit the possibil-

ity seemed more like a determination to convince herself. The look of terror on her face only convinced him she needed his help.

"You've never had a dream that seemed a bit too real?"

"Everyone does that." She shrugged.

"About murder?"

He'd struck a chord. She might not understand what could have been happening to her for several years, but he did. He'd seen it with other witnesses when the trauma began to wear off or another happened. Maybe Joseph had noticed.

"Words, motions, sounds, smells…they all work with the subconscious, Jolene. You heard the man yell 'gun.' Why didn't you move? Can you remember?"

"What do you mean? He yelled and you knocked me down the next second. I'll be bruised for days." She rubbed her shoulder, but her confusion was commonplace when blocking traumatic events.

"That's not what happened."

"Of course it is. You're overreacting." She shook her head, frowned, rubbed her chin, began to chew on her nail, then wrapped her arms around her middle to still her hands.

He could see the fright, see her chest rise and fall faster. Outside, the rain eased up to let the sun poke through the clouds. Levi saw the greenest eyes he'd come face-to-face with sparkle as they filled with tears.

"It's there, isn't it? A memory just out of reach."

"I was inside a toy box. My mother was stabbed to death downstairs. I couldn't have seen it." Her eyes closed as she dropped her face into her hands again. "My father saw it, but not me. I didn't." Her voice ended on a whisper.

"Jolene, I've read the report and I don't think you know what really happened. You've convinced yourself you

didn't see anything which was fine when you were five."
He used two fingers under her chin to draw her gaze back
to his eyes. "I can't protect you until you remember."

The tears came for real. She covered her face with her
hands and in the tiny space of the front seat, pulled her
knees to her chest and shrank into a ball.

Maybe he should hold and comfort her, but he snagged
her phone instead. It was safer. He really wanted to wrap
his arms around her shivering body and warm her up.
The urge to hold her confused him because he wanted to
keep holding her.

Not a good idea.

Before she'd left home, the one time he'd allowed himself to get that close had resulted in an ill-timed kiss. He
still wasn't certain who initiated what, but it hadn't been
a good idea then and was a terrible idea now.

"I'll give you a few minutes while I change the reser-
vations and take care of some details."

Trying to be patient and talk her around to his point of
view wasn't working. She would come around when the
reality of the situation hit her. She had to. She didn't have
a choice. But just in case she thought it would be a good
time to take off on her own, he switched the car off and
took the keys before he left her alone.

Levi sat on the trunk of the vehicle in the drizzle left
from the storm. He couldn't get any wetter. His jaws ached
from grinding his teeth. Proof that the decision he'd made
had been difficult and large. It wasn't about to get any easier by cutting himself off from the support he'd had over
the past eight years.

Jolene's cell allowed him to change her reservation
with the airline. Too easy. He also sent a text to her work
supervisor—the number clearly identified by scrolling
through her history. Also too easy.

"Sweet Mother."

If anyone obtained her phone information, they'd have her entire life at their fingertips. His gut twisted at the thought of what they'd do to her. What might have happened if he'd just released the body and not attended the funeral.

Removing the battery, he checked for "extra" electronics that may have been added by the men who wanted her dead. Nothing he could find, but it didn't mean they weren't there or that they hadn't simply cloned her phone.

Watching through the window, his witness who wasn't a witness had stopped crying. He walked from the car facing the ramp they'd used to the roof, keeping an eye out for a black sedan. One phone call, then he could get moving again, get her safe. But that one phone call might change his life.

*Might? Try would.*

He could ask himself why. Grind his teeth a little more and debate it. Or just hit his speed dial and get it over with. He shoved her phone in his pocket and pulled out his own.

"Hey, Levi, what happened? You didn't check in today." Sherry Peachtree had answered on the first ring, still at the office, still his commanding officer for at least five more minutes.

"Someone took a shot at Jolene Atkins this afternoon. The letter the Department of Justice sent and the one I brought in from Joseph said—"

"I know what the letters stated. I also remember you were told it wasn't a matter for the Marshal Service."

"I gave my word."

Silence. He felt obliged to fill it, justifying his reasons for pursuing. Trying one more time for approval. He didn't understand why Sherry could compel him to do anything, but filling the silence had been the case since they'd met.

"I knew Joseph. He wouldn't have written a letter unless Jolene were in serious danger."

"By writing a letter, he *put* his daughter in danger. We've already attempted to bring her into the program." In the background a door opened, then a muffled voice confirmed the department shouldn't be involved. "You know the DoJ can't prosecute without a reliable witness. You need to walk away."

"Not gonna happen."

"If things go badly…"

"They won't."

"They will. And we can't help you," she said.

He could lose everything or fulfill his promise to protect Joseph's daughter. "I figured as much. This decision already cost the life of one witness."

"Jolene Atkins is not a witness and you have no proof of foul play in her father's accident."

Silence.

He wouldn't fill it this time. There was no need. He'd already said what he had to say.

"I'll approve your request to extend your leave, escort her home and fly back to Denver. That's all I can do. You're on your own."

Silence. This time she'd disconnected.

"Damn it."

"I'd like to see the letter, please."

He knew the voice was Jolene's, but that didn't stop his hand from automatically going to his weapon as he swung around. He didn't draw it, but her eyes were focused on his sidearm.

"Later. We've got to get moving."

"You're assuming that I'm coming with you."

"Yes, I am."

"I wasn't in the toy box, was I?" She sounded sad and defeated.

Had she accepted things weren't as they seemed? He wanted to reach out and lend her some courage. More so than in the car. He couldn't. Instead he walked toward the rental, asking a question he knew she had only one response to.

"Coming?"

JOLENE PEERED AT the last-minute passengers boarding the train. She was careful to stay out of a direct view through the window, looking through the opening in the drawn curtains. Her escort had pulled them closed but she felt so confined she needed to see a larger space, an open area. She'd separated them a couple of inches.

She needed the train to move. Leaving Levi's protection wasn't an option at the moment. She'd been taught there were certain precautions to take when you disappeared. The first and foremost was to use cash for everything. Her emergency stash was in a safe in her apartment. All she had was a credit card and driver's license unless they made a withdrawal from her inheritance money.

Another reason to stay was to find answers. After being lied to for the past four years, she still believed Levi even though she couldn't remember hearing a gunshot this morning. Something pulled at her mind, a dark place that shouted, "Danger! Danger!" She didn't want to return, but somehow that place was the key to having any type of a normal life.

Her father had never visited in the two years since she'd left home. Each time she'd asked, he'd had an excuse. The flu, car trouble, papers at his job, home repairs… all sounded like legitimate reasons. His favorite excuse

was that old habits were hard to break. Day trips were all they'd managed—never far from Boulder.

So she'd gone home, met at the Denver airport both times by Levi. Driven in his black SUV, obviously an "office" vehicle. He'd taken precautions and she'd been blind. It was easy to believe the past no longer had control over her life.

Fantasy is easy.

Reality is not.

Where did that leave her? Part of a fictional life as a business assistant or the reality of a witness with no memory? Thinking about it made her head spin.

Seemingly ordinary travelers wandered the platform. A woman in a large hat caught her attention. Sleek, heels, beautiful, no luggage. Did that stranger have a *mundane* life? It had been extremely easy to fall into a false security of "normal" while living on her own.

Every person who boarded the train could be the one hired to kill her. No age or gender restrictions. Nothing could be taken for granted. She longed to throw the curtains wide and see if anyone cared.

Anyone other than Levi.

Oh, goodness. She knew that answer. A relationship wasn't possible. He was keeping a promise to her father. Protecting others was his job and he felt responsible. His concern wasn't on anything else.

Just thinking about being in the small rail compartment with him had her pulse racing. And if she weren't careful, she'd be salivating before he returned. So don't think of Levi. She could add that to her growing *Don't List*.

Impossible.

Especially overnight for the next fifteen hours.

The idea of sharing a close space with the most gorgeous man she'd ever known had been completely out of

her realm of imagination. But Levi Cooper hadn't been far from her thoughts since they'd met. She'd been comparing men to him for four years.

Somehow they were never as tall. Never as tan or much too thin. Their eyes were too close. Their noses didn't have the cute straightness that worked so well with the rest of his curved jaw. His dark hair was cute curled on his forehead, where on other men it was silly-looking. And none of them could wear a wet dress shirt like he could.

When he'd removed his coat, she wondered if the cotton had shrunk to form-fit the muscles across his arms and chest.

*Add 'don't watch Levi undress' to the Don't List.*

She took a deep breath, relaxed her shoulders and stretched her neck. She could do this.

Life with her father had always been a list of *don'ts*. Her father had drilled it into her head to be safe. Don't get too far from home. Don't be out of cell range. Don't go anywhere alone. Don't write letters. Don't forget to check in. And most importantly—don't make friends.

Perhaps that's why it had been so easy to accept that her father had been released from WITSEC. Levi was introduced as a friend and their friendly relationship seemed to have been encouraged.

Naïve. She'd been so naïve. But no longer.

None of it was real. The two men in her life had shared a secret and that hurt most of all.

But she could hold on to her own secrets. Levi might think he knew about the nightmares, but she wouldn't admit anything. If she focused, she could keep the details to herself. She'd never share how the dream about a white room was streaked with red. She seemed to look through fog and dark red would be everywhere.

She couldn't lie to herself any longer and claim it was

just her imagination fabricating a part of her mother's death. Or that it was a dream she'd thought couldn't possibly be related to anything real. Until this afternoon.

Not a dream at all. The rest of the images were fuzzy, blurred to where she couldn't take a guess at what they represented. What had she seen when the man had yelled "gun"? The harder she tried to focus, the less clear it became.

"You won't get home faster by clicking your ruby-red slippers and making a wish."

"I didn't hear you."

"That's becoming a habit."

"Please stop lecturing and let's eat." She lifted the stowaway table, but he put his hands on top of hers. Levi had instructed her to stay put and had supposedly gone in search of food. His hands were empty.

"You sure you don't want a shower first?" he asked.

"No food?"

"Dining car isn't serving until we get underway."

"And you aren't sharing where you really went." She began to lift the table again. "So let's look at the letter."

He smiled and shook his head.

"You're not going to show me the letter until the train is moving." She dropped the tray into its slot and relaxed on the couch again, pulling her feet under her, not caring about her muddy, damp clothing. It was his bed. "You're afraid I won't stay? Levi, I have nowhere else to go. You're stuck with me a while."

"Very perceptive."

"Not normally." The facts of her parents' deaths evaded her. She'd been duped by the two closest people in her life. No, she wasn't feeling very smart at the moment.

"I'll feel a bit more comfortable once we're out of St. Louis," he said.

"It's been an exhausting day." She just didn't have the energy to think about anything. She tucked a pillow by her ear, propping herself up against the wall, trying her best to stay awake. She closed her eyes. "This conversation is taking too much effort."

*Gun!*

*She heard the word through a fog on a hillside. What had happened to the rain? A rainbow shattered, splintering through the white. Something. She tried to grab hold. A face? A...what was it? Remember. She had to remember. But if she did, she'd get hurt. Mama told her...she said not to say a word. What is it? She's so close. Remember. Don't...remember.*

"Dad!"

She'd shouted herself awake. The ker-thunk she felt in her chest was her heart, not the train. She rubbed away the sleep and what little makeup might have remained on her eyes.

"You okay?" Levi stood bare-chested directly in front of her.

"Yeah. Fine."

"Bad dream?" he asked with that knowing smile of his.

"I think so. This is so silly. I should be able to remember. I just woke up."

"Don't rush it. You only drifted off a few minutes." He stood, stretching his arms to the overhead compartment where he'd stowed his duffel bag.

His muscles grew taut and he may have sucked in his gut. She wasn't certain, but it was nice to think he was showing off. Even endorphins couldn't shake the eerie feeling from the dream. She needed to move more than the two feet available in the compartment. "When is the train going to leave?"

"Any minute. We can talk about your dream." Levi stretched a white undershirt over his head.

"No talking. Not yet."

She tried to dart to the side, make it to the corner before he could move again, but bad timing chose that moment for the train to ease into motion. She fell against his body. His bare arms quickly wrapped her in a protective embrace, leaving the shirt stuck around his neck. Her hot cheek pressed against the smooth cool skin of his shoulder.

"It's okay, Jolene."

The way his hand skimmed her hair and the back of her neck, soothed her like a drug. She could become addicted very quickly to this level of comfort. Her hands found the natural curves of the muscles in his back. The same ones she'd wanted to explore earlier through his wet shirt.

The vibration of the train made her toes tingle, at least that was the most logical explanation. If she didn't have that reasoning, then she was tingly all over because he was holding her.

Oh, no. Not again. He'd think she'd done it on purpose, to get close to him. There was no way to explain what had been happening in her head without talking.

No talking. No explanations. Not yet.

In her current state of exhaustion, she'd lose her concentration. Before she knew it, she'd be sitting back in a hypnotherapist's chair or with a psychiatrist attempting to "clear her mind."

She jumped away from him as quickly as she'd landed there. She just should have left before her hands had wandered around his strong sinewy back. One step and the couch was against her knees. Not far enough.

"I'm sorry, I should have waited." She pointed toward the bath door. "I just…you know, needed to use the sink."

"Jolene…"

She couldn't let him talk or touch her. She sidestepped his body and shuffled to the sink to splash water on her face. *Stay awake. Keep it together. Just ignore him until he shares answers.* He moved toward the window, slipping the curtain open an inch with that long finger that had slid over the curve of her collarbone.

It couldn't be happening again. She refused to believe she still had a crush on the handsome Levi Cooper. She'd been over him a long time.

He was larger than anything in her dull life. Full of energy, fun, confidence.

Hold on, that was all fake. He'd lied. She needed to get her head on straight and had a horrible feeling it wasn't going to happen anytime soon.

*Fifteen hours on a train? In a room just with him?*

Quickly locking the door to the two-foot shower/toilet, she had every intention of never coming out or facing him again. Especially in Dallas.

# Chapter Three

LEVI STARED AT the door and absently polished his weapon with his T-shirt. It was the best he could do without a cleaning kit. Something to keep him awake, alert, prepared. They were on a train, had been for almost six hours.

He didn't like unknowns and there were a heck of a lot of them associated with Joseph, Elaine and Jolene Atkins. Protection duty was a lot different than investigative work.

*I hope I don't let you down, Joseph.*

Jolene had come out of the shower an hour after he'd promised an extra large T-shirt. The steward didn't have a problem collecting one from the souvenir shop or a couple of burgers from the dining car. After all, it was an emergency with their "lost" luggage. The fifty he'd given him earlier to keep an eye on anyone lurking around and report back to him had helped.

Sheer exhaustion had finally put Jolene to sleep a couple of hours ago. He'd have to doze eventually, but not until the train passed through Little Rock, Arkansas, around 3:00 a.m. He reloaded silently, verifying with each bul-

let there was no residue from his encounter with the mud hole at the funeral.

One day, they'd visit Joseph's gravesite when the sun shone and she could have a peaceful memory to keep.

Hell, there wouldn't be a "one day" for them. Not together. If they got involved, it would just get messy and confusing.

It was imperative that Jolene regain her memories and enter WITSEC. When she did, she'd be reassigned. Whisked away without a goodbye. Like had happened to so many of his witnesses over the past eight years.

No remorse. Or none that she could know about. She needed a new life free from these monsters who had taken both parents from her. He'd seen the file on what the murderers had done to her mother, to the protection detail and to Joseph himself.

The little girl from those photos hadn't spoken for weeks. She'd shown all the symptoms of PTSD. When her dad had been released from the hospital, she'd begun to bounce back. No report of any memory of the event.

"Is something wrong?" Jolene whispered from the top berth.

"Nope," he whispered across the small room.

At this speed there weren't too many lights passing by the window, just enough to see the tousled hair, the sleepy eyes, the question of whether to be afraid. Enough for her to notice he wasn't wearing a shirt. Enough for him to see the attraction reflected in her eyes.

"Why are you still awake then?" she asked.

"Can't sleep. You should though. You need to be alert tomorrow." He kept his voice low, not wanting to disturb any chance she had of returning to pleasant dreams. So he continued to whisper, keeping it quiet, enjoying her

sultry voice when she reciprocated. He slid his gun back in its holster.

She tried to sit, but since there wasn't room she slowly maneuvered over the bunk's edge. The T-shirt rose higher, making him wish he was on his berth with a closer view. Lord have mercy, he'd forgotten how much he enjoyed looking at her legs.

No, he hadn't. He had *no* problem recalling that dangerous memory.

No more dangerous than him realizing there was nothing under that shirt and showing enough backside that…

*Definitely time to think about something else.*

"Listen, Levi, I don't want you to get the idea that I'm a complete dolt."

"What?" Had she caught him looking? "Why would I?"

*A little upset, buried your father today, alone in a world that's turned upside down, sexy as a supermodel…but never a dolt.*

"I stayed in the bathroom over an hour." She settled, pulling his pillow under her arm to lean on, tugging at the blanket to cover her legs. Driving him insane with how vulnerable she appeared.

He thought about flipping on the lights. He'd be able to see her better, but she'd have the same advantage. And he didn't know if the desire probably written on his face was good for her to see. A tension he felt everywhere, all the time. Looking at her, he knew he couldn't hide it.

"You had your reasons."

"Not good ones." She shrugged.

"I'm not complaining, Jo." He quickly pulled the undershirt over his head and arms. *Safer this way.* "It's been a long day with a lot to take in. So why don't you grab some more shuteye. You can stay in my berth. I won't be using it."

"I need to see the letter."

"Now? At one in the morning?"

"Yes. I'm ready. I wasn't before, but I am now." She rushed the last bit, but there was a calm in her voice that helped him believe her. And the fact she stuck her chin in the air, sort of challenging him to think differently.

It had been risky not opening the letter earlier. Everything in his training said to do it, not leave anything to chance. But he had to trust his instinct about Joseph. *If*— and that was a huge if—he'd discovered who had killed his wife he would have turned over the information immediately to the Department of Justice. His letter to Levi indicated that much. He said he'd know when to give her the wood carving from the house and assured him the letter was personal, to let her read it only when she was calm.

Now was good.

Jolene could read the message, react to it here, hopefully trust him and the WITSEC program. They'd reach Dallas, he'd turn the matter over to the DoJ, make certain Jolene was protected and he'd return to his life.

He retrieved the letters from his duffel, leaving the dog statue—and its instructions—for later. One letter addressed to Witness Security, one to himself and one unopened addressed to Jolene.

"I have no idea what's inside your envelope. I respected your dad's wishes, kept it secure and delivered it to you."

"I wasn't expecting… You didn't mention there was one for me."

"He instructed me not to. Asked me to hand deliver it." He sat next to her, half wanting to be near, half needing to look over her shoulder and read the letter. "Are you sure you're up for this now?"

"Positive."

He handed over her envelope. She carefully peeled

back the flap while he flipped the reading lamp on be-hind her head.

Silence. Except for the recurring sounds of the pas-senger cars rolling over the tracks. A regular beat to calm his racing pulse. The thought about opening her letter had crossed his mind more than once in the last four days. If he leaned just a bit closer he could see it. Instead, he leaned forward, propping his elbows on his knees—avoiding the temptation.

Both the message and Jolene.

The letters had arrived Special Delivery from an un-known source—he suspected a lawyer. Whoever it was had covered their tracks well.

The Marshals Service document was a copy delivered indirectly through the Department of Justice. The DoJ might have more luck finding the lawyer, but with Joseph's death and no other witness, it wasn't a high priority. Until Jolene read her letter, Levi hadn't wanted to push for more involvement from either department that had declined to authorize protection.

He tilted his head to watch her, ready if she needed him. He didn't care how awkward it might make things in the morning. He couldn't sit by and watch her hurt…alone.

Tears rolled down her cheeks. Her thumbnail went back to her chin. An old habit she'd been attempting to break since high school. Her thumbnail dug into the cute little cleft, sometimes spending more time scraping along her lower lip. He didn't know why she tried so hard to stop. He liked it.

She read. A very long letter. Turning the pages back and forth several times once she was done. Looking up to him for something—he didn't know what she expected.

"What did yours say?" she asked, no longer whisper-ing, but with a voice choked with tears.

"We could swap."

"Actually, we can't. Mine was a private goodbye and apology. It had nothing to do with Mama, you or men threatening my life."

"Obviously, I'd hoped for something different." *More clues to who was behind everything would have helped, Joseph.*

"The letter please?" She held out one hand and with the other used the edge of the blanket to dry her eyes. "Never mind. Can you read it aloud?"

He nodded and leaned against the wall, bringing the letter closer to her, needing the light from behind her shoulder. He wanted to lift his arm, tuck her into his side, have her lean on him while she listened.

Too dangerous.

He could almost recite the letter from memory, having gone over it a hundred times since its arrival. She needed to hear all the words. He lifted a page and read.

"'I'm sorry to place the responsibility of looking after Jo on you, Levi, but you know there's no one else. You can get into a lot of trouble for what I'm asking, but my little girl needs your help and protection.

"'Over the years, I mentioned that I should have died that day, but I hung on for Jolene. That of course is the truth, but I also yearned for revenge. It should have been justice, but as a husband and father, I don't try to fool myself.

"'Four years ago you respected my wishes and introduced yourself as a friend. Since that time, the lie has become truth and I consider you family. By now you know I've pleaded with the Department of Justice to bring Jolene into the program. Jolene needs you. There's evidence locked away in her memories. And I'm afraid I made a horrible mistake allowing her to move away from us. Her

memories are beginning to surface even if she doesn't recognize them. You're the only one I trust to take care of her.'"

When he looked up from the page, her palm was extended. He handed it over, as expected.

"So there's nothing in your letter, either."

"I have a second page," he said, and reached to the empty side of the berth for page two. He dreaded reading it to her. The short-lived camaraderie was about to end. She may explode, run, hate him. He'd believed the letter, believed in Joseph and believed in Jolene. She'd come around. She didn't have to like him to accept his protection.

"'If you're receiving this note with your letter, Levi, it means we didn't have a chance to meet after my return. I've been too bold, too careless and exposed my Atkins identity to the wrong people. Perhaps I should have just called you, but I don't trust anything any longer.

"'My absences have been following recent information that finally led me to something solid. I've never stopped searching for those who destroyed my family. I've discovered why my wife's testimony was such a threat to her client. Her enemy is even more powerful after twenty years. I would turn over what I know to the Department of Justice now, but they refuse to help Jo. I had no choice but to return to Boulder. I hope she can forgive me.'"

He had to swallow, dreading the last paragraph.

"'You can't tell Jo until she's safely in your care. I wish I could say everything I've done is only so my daughter can have a real life, but it's also for Elaine. Jo's letter, let her share it with you when she's ready. I hope you'll respect my wishes. Thank you, my friend, and farewell.'"

The first page crumpled in her fist. He placed his hand over hers but she threw it off, jumping up, wrapping her arms around her slim waist.

"He…he was… Oh, my God. They murdered him. Why didn't you tell me? Tell anyone? What was he thinking?"

He'd been thinking like a friend, respecting the wishes of a man he admired. Not thinking like a U.S. Marshal. Deep down if he admitted the truth, he'd thought Joseph was a bit paranoid and he hadn't believed the contents of his letter until the shot had been fired at the funeral.

"You should have told me."

"You're probably right. Hand delivering the letter was a part of my instructions. Maybe not my smartest move. I trusted your dad. I should have trusted him more, not less. Turns out his suspicions were right."

"This changes everything. Are they investigating the accident? No, not an accident—murder. Both of my parents were murdered." She turned to all the walls, felt her clothes drying in the shower area, paced back to the window and dropped her forehead against the glass. "Why can't I remember anything?"

He stood so fast he clipped his shoulder on the top berth frame, a sting that couldn't compare to what Jo must be feeling. Before he could reach out and try to take her in his arms she turned on him. Defenseless kitten into wild mountain cat.

"Why are you here? You're the only person who knows the truth. You should be investigating his murder, not babysitting me." She shoved passed him—not far since the compartment wouldn't allow it.

"I did check." He knew this would happen. At least she wasn't shouting. One of the reasons he'd wanted the train moving when she read the letter was to keep her by his side. "There was no indication of foul play. When I retrieved your father's body, I asked the local Sheriff's Department to give the scene and car another onceover."

"And?"

"I haven't heard anything yet."

"What is the Marshals Service doing?"

"They can't do anything, Jolene." That caged mountain cat was growing more edgy, rubbing her palms, tugging at the bottom of the T-shirt. "You can't, either. Not here."

She stopped, directly under his chin, looking at his shirt.

"This is ridiculous, Levi. They received a letter. What did it say?" Her voice was calm again.

Level, but demanding. Her fingernail tapped on his chest like it normally did her chin. He wanted to grab her hand—not to stop the tapping, just because. There wasn't a reason and that made it very unsafe to stop the tapping.

"Joseph said you were in danger and needed to be protected." He braced himself for a slap, shove, a reaction to his next words. "They considered it a last-ditch effort to get you in the program by a lonely dad."

"They didn't think it coincidental that he'd died?" She shoved at his chest and crossed to the compartment door. "And they aren't concerned because I'm not legally their problem."

"Come on, Jo, what do you expect? That letter was the first time your father had spoken about you to the Service in almost ten years. No one had any idea why he'd sent it. No one at the Service or the DoJ had any idea your dad was looking into the case himself."

"No one?" she asked, her voice quivered with doubt and humiliation—maybe because she'd been excluded.

"Not even me." He stayed his ground, ready to yank her away from the door if she tried to run. He wouldn't blame her. She was hurting. He understood how much. "If I had known I would have stopped him. He knew that."

"He gave up everything. Lost everything…"

"Not everything, Jo." As gently as possible, he turned

her around and brought her close to his chest. He should never think twice about bringing her closer to him, but that wasn't their life. They were friends. More of a relationship wasn't possible.

"Stop." She pushed him away.

He released his hold. One he had no right to.

"You can't keep doing that. I can't depend on anyone but myself." Her knuckles turned white grabbing the small sink counter. "You taught me that two years ago."

"I know." It didn't matter what he'd wanted or didn't want. "You were the daughter of a witness. Period."

"I can't trust you to tell me everything. If you think it's for my better good, you'll…"

"You're right about that. I will protect you at all costs."

She hit the counter, tears overflowing from her eyes. "As soon as we get off this train, I want you to leave me alone."

"Not gonna happen."

"I'll hire a private detective to find out about my family. Hire my own bodyguards."

"Don't be ridiculous. You don't have enough money to fight the 'powerful' enemy your Dad refers to."

She looked lost and frustrated, using her sleeve to swipe at her cheeks. "I'm serious about you leaving me alone." Her eyes darted first to her clothes, then shoes, where she'd stuck her phone and small wallet she'd had in her jacket.

But the battery was in his duffel.

"Don't even think about leaving. You can't do this on your own. That's why your father sent me. I mean it, Jo." The room was small. He only lifted an arm and touched her shoulder. "You need my help and I'm giving it. No strings attached."

"You made that very clear two years ago."

HOW HAD HE gotten himself into this mess? No partner. No backup. No information.

Levi splashed some water on his face and scrubbed it dry with a towel. No use looking in the mirror, the compartment was too dark. Couldn't talk to himself or exercise, he'd wake Jolene.

*Think.*

He was tired of thinking. He'd done nothing but think since the letters had arrived. He'd been certain her private letter would sort things out. Point the finger at someone, somewhere to start an investigation.

Nothing. Joseph had lost his life. Jolene had been shot at, might still be compromised. And he'd probably lose his job and the ability to investigate further.

How was he supposed to keep her safe if she refused to remember? That was all they had, their only chance. Return to the scene of the crime, where the murders had taken place and pray the images became clear in her mind.

In fact, Joseph had been certain the visit would trigger her memories. Levi could see now that many of their conversations over the past six months had been feeding him information he could use to help Jo through this threat.

He'd find out nine hours from now. But he couldn't do anything at the moment. Not this tired.

They'd passed through Little Rock and his witness hadn't tried to leave. She'd promised, but he hadn't trusted her. Something about her acceptance of his assistance bothered him, put his senses on high alert.

*Stop thinking.*

It was time to grab some shuteye. He checked the locked door one last time and shifted the outside window curtains so just a sliver of moonbeam lit the bed. With his holster on his hip, he turned in the chair until he found a halfway

decent position. Better to doze uncomfortably than fall into a dead state of exhaustion.

Besides, he wasn't squeezing his torso onto the smaller upper berth and wasn't waking Jo to move her back to it. His eyes had barely shut when something pushed his brain into gear.

A small foot peeked out from under the covers. Jolene's back was to him. No way to tell if she was awake or still in slumber land. He kept his lids slightly parted to see what she'd do.

Did she really think she could get away from him on a train? Where would she hide?

The compartment lock turned.

Key.

Not Jo. Not the steward.

He wanted to let whoever threatened inside, catch them, eliminate the danger.

Not alone. He had to protect Jo who was vulnerable in that bunk. He shouldn't have put the vest away with his gear.

He shot across the room as soundlessly as he could, pulled Jo on top of him on the floor, covering her mouth as she woke. As best as his six-two form could manage, he rolled her beneath him to protect from an assault.

He recognized the momentary panic in her eyes that quickly subsided, shifting to question.

Shh. He mouthed the age-old sign to be quiet and braced for an attack.

Where was the shot?

The door had slid inches, but no one entered.

He lowered his mouth to her ear. "I'm going to move toward the berths and you're going into the shower."

She nodded and they repositioned. He quickly got to his back with his gun pointed toward the door.

Nothing.

"Could it have been someone who had the wrong compartment?" she whispered a minute later.

"Door was locked."

She stared through the three-inch opening. "What does this mean?"

"Whoever's trying to kill you…is on this train."

## Chapter Four

Jolene crouched on the floor of the shower watching Levi's arm muscles lock into place. He was on his back near the bunk, chin on his chest, gun pointed toward the passageway door, steady as a rock, barely breathing.

Ridiculous to think he was sexy, but that was the word.

She tugged her clothes off the shower nozzle and into her arms. She looked up in time to catch her protector move his head from side to side. No? Well, they'd at least be in her possession if they moved.

He mouthed at her to stay quiet. She interpreted his head motion and backed into the four-foot rectangle called a bathroom. They waited silently in the dark, out of each other's sight, for what seemed hours. Reality was only minutes. She counted her heartbeats so she wouldn't talk.

Levi finally moved. She heard him perfectly through the wall only as thick as an office partition. The compartment door slid shut, the lock turned, switches flipped back and forth.

"No lights. The call button doesn't work," he said in a deep, low voice.

"Aren't you going after them?" she asked in the lowest whisper she could manage.

"And get shot when I head down the stairwell?"

"Aren't there two ways down from this level?" she asked and scooted forward until she could see him.

"We don't know how many threats there are." He kicked away his duffel that blocked the shower door, put his back to the wall, gun toward the threat.

"There's got to be some way around them." She was thinking aloud. Brainstorming. Trying at least.

"Like how? You want me to go out a window that probably doesn't open, pull myself on top of a moving train at full-speed, climb down between the passenger cars and fight an unknown assassin bold enough to attack us in our compartment?"

"Sounds reasonable. Men do it all the time in the movies."

"Right. I'm not stupid, Jo. And I won't risk your life by leaving you alone."

"I was kidding." She stood, straightening her cramped legs, hoping Mr. Sexy would let her leave the increasingly smaller shower area. One shake of his head nixed that idea. It wasn't ideal and completely embarrassing, but she sat on the toilet seat, wrapping the towel over her thighs. At least it was dark.

"The attack is so farfetched it doesn't make sense. What did they want to accomplish?" He shoved his gun into its holster and pushed the steward call button again. "They must want to lure me away from the room or they would have shot us dead through the door. I won't make it that easy for them. Bottom line—I'm not leaving your side."

"Then what do we do?"

"You're staying in the shower 'til we get to Dallas."

She hadn't been serious last night when she'd thought she'd hide in this part of the room the entire trip. "Now, you're the one kidding."

"No, Jo, I'm not."

His voice had a perfect calm to it, the one she recog-

nized as a U.S. Marshal taking command. Finding out his occupation explained so much about his actions, the way he spoke, stood, seemed to have eyes that watched everything. Including her.

A look she recognized and had interpreted as interest when she'd lived at home. She'd resented his arbitrary dismissal of their attraction two years ago. In spite of their current circumstances, she still wondered what it would have been like.

Oh, bother! None of it would matter if they didn't get out of their train compartment alive.

"Why wouldn't they just shoot us?" she asked to get her mind back on the situation.

"Killing a Marshal on a train would draw a lot of attention."

"And they don't want attention," she added. "You said no one knew your connection to my dad, but, Levi, how would they know you're a marshal?"

"Dammit," he whispered angrily into the darkness. "We've been compromised." He stood, looking taller than ever backlit from the small amount of moonlight.

The door slammed in her face. She swallowed a split second of panic at the dark, but she closed her eyes and imagined her college dorm room where she'd gotten dressed without waking her roommates lots of mornings.

So she did. She quickly pulled on her slacks. All the while hearing several savory curse words through the door. He wasn't pleased. Assuming the coast was still clear, she stuck her head around the small dividing wall. "Mind telling me what's going on?"

She sat in the chair. A look from him and she moved to the floor in front of the bathroom.

He moved to the door, pistol barrel pulling the curtain. Angrier than she'd ever seen him. A smidgen of light from

the hallway caressed his frowning face, furrowed with thought and concern for her safety. She knew him or at least a part of him.

"Compromised? You could begin there," she said.

"When they killed your father, they must have waited for his body to be claimed. I identified myself as a marshal. They've known who I was all along. I led them straight to you."

"Oh." Fear clogged her throat. There really was no going back. No return to the life she'd had in Georgia as a nonessential assistant, searching websites. No return to her father's home under the protection of Levi.

"I can only assume they waited until they thought we were both asleep," he said.

She was in over her head and completely defenseless, with the exception of Levi. A secret weapon she didn't know about herself until a few hours ago. Having him close was a line of security she needed, but was also comforted by.

"Good thing you weren't asleep."

He raised an eyebrow. Instead of the smile that normally accompanied one of her wrong conclusions, his lips flattened. "They must have heard me drag you to the floor and changed their minds."

"Then we're very lucky." She did feel fortunate. She couldn't have been facing this alone, but Levi was there and determined to protect her.

"How do you figure that? We still don't know who *they* are and we're stuck on a dang train."

"That's right." The fear had eased. She had a secret weapon—Levi. "We don't know who they are, but at least we know they're here."

FROM THE ONE spot on the floor Levi let her occupy, Jolene watched him poised on the bottom berth. Whoever chased

them would have to be a fool to face Levi now that he was prepared for their return.

She on the other hand, needed to stand and stretch, but the only place he allowed her to do so was inside the shower. Looking at the drain in the floor had gotten old—fast. She sat on a pillow ready to dive into the stall if there was another incident. He stared at the locked door, barely moving, acknowledging her ideas for leaving, but not divulging much about his plans.

No matter what scenario she'd thought up, he reasonably explained why they should stay where they were. He kept his back to the window, gun at the tip of his fingers, looking completely cool and comfortable.

Only one thing made her more frustrated. Come to think about it, she could blame Levi for that one, too.

"This is ridiculous." She'd mumbled on purpose. She admitted the desire to irritate him just a tad and mumbling had always irritated him.

"You say that a lot."

"Well, that's the way I feel. We can't just sit here and wait any longer."

He didn't bother to answer. She knew that look of "why not?" He'd been throwing it in her direction for the past hour.

"What if *they* come back?" she asked for the tenth time.

His finger tapped his gun.

Growing up she'd seen guns with other marshals and didn't feel anxious when Levi handled his. If he fired, she hoped he hit his target and no stray bullets went through the walls.

"And then what, Levi? There's nowhere to hide. No bathtub or wall thick enough to stop their bullets. I feel like a cornered mouse in a deathtrap."

"We've discussed that we can't predict what they'll do or where they'll strike. Isn't it safer to just stay here?"

"I've been talking and you don't like any of my ideas, especially the version of just calling your boss. So why don't *you* answer your question this time? If you were the bad guys, why try to get into our room an hour ago?"

She watched his eyes narrow, how his fingers stroked the stubble on his chin, then switched to a brief scratch. His brown eyes were a rich deep chocolate, reminding her how hungry she was. Not only for food, but also for the closeness they'd shared. She missed that.

*Does he realize that his fingers are a gentle caress every time he even casually touches me?*

He swung his legs over the edge of the berth and faced her. "Make the hits while everyone's asleep, return to my seat, stay put, exit next stop. Our dead bodies aren't discovered until it's time to debark in Dallas."

"And when that didn't work, what would your next move be?" she asked.

"I'd wait until we were closer to a town, where the train slows, make the hit, then jump."

"Then we should change that plan by getting out of this room." She wasn't a claustrophobic person. Not normally anyway, but she'd be better not being in a six-by-six foot room for a while. "We need to think of something they won't expect."

"And not get killed in the process." He half grinned. "One thing's for certain, when our steward comes around we're getting out of this 'deathtrap' of a room." His eyes twinkled, repeating her description.

"The call button still doesn't work."

"He's already been tipped to show up at five-thirty." He glanced at his watch. "Fifteen minutes. We're getting off in Texarkana."

"Levi Cooper, you knew what you were going to do all along."

"And if I did?"

"I can handle the truth, you know."

"Never doubted you could," he said, holstering his gun.

Remembering how he'd kissed her goodbye didn't help calm her scorching insides.

If he'd revealed he was a marshal four years ago, perhaps the thought of becoming involved wouldn't have entered her head. His simple "we can't do this" hadn't stopped her from thinking about him or wondering what she'd done wrong.

Good grief, she could admit that he was just plain handsome, but not the guy for her. She was tired of sharing only half-truths and being unable to say she didn't like roller coasters or speed boats or even watching race cars. She couldn't answer why because it led to the life of a woman who never grew past the age of five.

A woman whose headstone she'd come face-to-face with the day before.

The most appealing part of this very moment was honesty. Being with Levi meant no secrets, no more lies about herself.

And yet, she knew he still held something back. She'd gained a lot of perspective since leaving her father's watchful, concerned eyes.

"Why didn't you tell me your plan?"

He stood, stretched, shrugged. Stepped across the room to offer her a hand to help her stand. She took it, stayed where she was, waiting for him to answer.

"Your other choice was to have me distract you with a kiss. This has been the longest conversation we've had without disagreeing in two years. You've been full of ideas and finally came around to the one I liked. If I had to im-

provise, then we'd have to go through everything again. Anyway, you respond better if it's your idea."

He didn't slow down at her shocked reaction to his suggested kiss idea. A kiss? He'd thought about kissing her?

"I cannot believe you just said that."

He tugged her to her feet with his firm grasp on her hand. He didn't stop there and circled her with an embrace. She was ready for this. Ready to feel his firm lips on hers again. To see if it was everything she remembered.

"You said you could take the truth," he said in a voice full with desire.

"If we're being so truthful… Why did you kiss me at the airport before I left for Georgia? You'd said there was no way—"

Levi brought a finger to her lips, then he swirled it to her chin, tilting her face until their eyes met. "I kissed you because I couldn't *not* kiss you."

She remembered the firmness of his lips, the perfection of that one kiss. Or had she distorted the memory?

"And now? Are you going to *not* do it again?"

The time for talking ended and it didn't matter if Levi wanted to kiss her. *She* wanted to kiss him. She rose onto her toes, taking advantage of the small space and the exposed skin at his neck. His hands dropped away, quickly encircling her waist and back. He held her to his chest, barely letting her feet touch the floor.

They leaned together, meeting in the middle of the short space between them. Everything was the same. Her memory hadn't exaggerated the thrill of his mouth on hers at all. Waves of tingles took her to a place she didn't want to leave.

His hands skated under her loose T-shirt. When they connected with her skin, his light touch explored while he held her against his rock-hard body. He slowly released her

until her feet were on the floor. She enjoyed the firmness of the muscles in his arms she'd admired all day, wanting to discover more.

Wanting to discover more of his kisses.

A soft tap on the compartment window broke them apart.

"That would be Max and Dave, the stewards. You up for this?" he asked calmly.

Her insides were jumping, having nothing to do with the motion of the train speeding across the Arkansas tracks. He looked composed, but she placed a hand over his heart and felt it racing as fast as her own. Their eyes connected and she received his smile telling her she knew the real answer, no matter what he might say or do.

"Yes. Don't trust anyone and be ready for anything." She remembered that. The phrase had been drilled into her brain her entire life by her father. "You set this up before we left St. Louis?"

He nodded.

"You also reserved this compartment before—"

"Yeah, I did. Just in case. Before the train pulled out, I found long-term Amtrak employees. Two men I would recognize when they showed up. No chance of someone who might conveniently be replaced at the last minute."

They moved to the dining car without a problem or seeing another person. She sat on a bar stool as the stewards left.

"As frightened as I am, it is so good to be out of that room." Relief shot through her. "I am incredibly hungry and tired all at the same time." She wanted to stretch out in a bed and sleep for an entire day. Then wake up and see what possibilities there may be with Levi.

"Adrenaline's wearing off," he said.

"Is that why the train feels like it's slower?"

"No, it *is* slower. They're applying the brakes." For a split second, surprise flashed through Levi's eyes. He quickly hid it behind a screen of concentration. "Hear that?"

Faint shouting from the following passenger car, steadily grew louder. Screams. They were in the middle of nowhere. No town lights, just moonbeams on trees and cleared pastures. Miles from help.

"What's happening? Why are we stopping?"

"Fire!"

The word was muted through the door, but distinctive, not misunderstood.

"This can't be a coincidence," she said.

"It's not. Opening the compartment door must have been the plan to get us out in the open. They don't want you dead, Jo." He searched the room, still relatively empty. "The bastard wants something you have."

A chill washed over her. Something just out of reach. A glimpse to something dark…and then it was gone.

A family came through the door. The woman's fear for her children was clear in how tightly she held the youngest and the terrified glazed look in her eyes. Because Jo hadn't listened to Levi about the funeral, her parents' murderers set a train on fire.

"This is all my fault. People are going to be hurt. What if someone's—"

"Don't go there. You aren't responsible." He pulled the bulletproof vest from his duffel and looped the strap over her head and chest. "I should have put this on you before we left the compartment."

Levi was right. They hadn't started a fire today. She hadn't done anything except come into the kitchen when the adults were talking. She knew she could get in trouble, but she'd hurt her finger and needed Mama to fix it.

*Oh, my God.*

"Levi, I…"

He didn't hear her. The alarms were sounding. People had begun pouring into the dining car. The screams and crying drowned out almost everything else. She needed to hold on to the memory from when she was five and get off this train.

When they were safe, she could tell him about the rainbow nightmare. A crystal hanging in the window had splashed color all around the room for a few minutes every day. A strange man had a rainbow face. It was an incomprehensible memory, tangled in a child's imagination.

"Jo? Did you hear me?" Levi asked. He tilted his head down to her ear. "I think they want you alive. Don't freak out. The vest is just a precaution."

*I remembered the last time I saw Mama alive.* She wanted to scream the words so he'd know. So someone would know.

Levi was already on the bar, sliding over the counter. He motioned for her to do the same. She pulled her shoes off and followed, noticing he'd put the vest on her while she'd been inside her nightmare. He helped her to the floor, then took her by the shoulders, focused only on her.

"Don't leave my side, Jo. No matter what happens. Doesn't matter what you hear or who asks you for help. Promise."

"But—"

"No buts, Jo. Promise. Whoever's out to get you doesn't care about innocent lives or how many people get hurt. Remember that." He stretched a used, wet bar towel across her face. "When the train stops, we go out the door with you holding my belt. Got it?"

She could only nod. He planted himself between her

and the mass of people moving toward them on the other side of the bar counter.

People shoved trying to get closer to the door. The smoke poured into the car, gathering like a dangerous fog above their heads, slowly choking the air from the panicked crowd.

The train came to an abrupt stop and the rush of people stormed through. One of the stewards who had been so helpful earlier stumbled just to her left. The mob wouldn't stop. It took three men—one of them Levi—to block the flow long enough for the man to stand.

Breathing was horrible. No deep breaths like her lungs longed to do. Her eyes stung, watered, blurred. Holding on to Levi, she had only one hand to keep the wet towel over her nose and mouth.

Levi held his ground, not budging, letting the crush sweep past them. She turned her bare feet as flat to the wall as possible, but when the fourth or fifth person stepped on them, she screamed in pain, losing her towel.

"Stay with me."

She heard Levi's voice through the mob and didn't understand when he turned into the smoke. Forcing her aching feet to follow, she lost her grip on his belt and hooked her arm through the duffel strap.

More people kept pouring through the door.

"Where are you going?" a man in an Amtrak vest shouted at Levi. "There's no exit back there. All the other doors are locked and the dining car is the only way out."

Another man stepped on her foot, scraping her shin along the way. The pain was so great, Jolene couldn't stop the scream. Levi's hand swung back, connecting with her arm, giving it a slight squeeze. His assurance helped her hold on.

She stretched the collar of the T-shirt over her nose

and mouth. The smoke was thicker and made it difficult to see. She held tight to the duffel strap afraid of being the next person trampled, even if the crowd had thinned to mainly employees.

Then the green strap fell loose in her hand.

She stretched, shoving to get to him, missing his belt.

"Levi!" Her pathetic cry went unheeded. She could only manage a wheezing shout. She watched the duffel fall to the floor and Levi disappeared behind billowing black smoke. He had to know she wasn't there since his bag had dropped.

He'd follow. He'd find her. She could trust him.

The vest weighed her down. Her collar tugged at her neck, caught on something, choking her. She frantically jerked at it as she lurched away from Levi. The bottom of the shirt ripped and she took a deep smoky breath, stinging her throat, overpowering her lungs. Her eyes watered, but she could see the Amtrak vest inches in front of her.

The urge to drop to the floor for cleaner air was great, but she couldn't battle those trying to escape. She could no longer breathe in the dining car and had to get good air.

One second she'd been connected to Levi, feeling more secure headed toward the fire than safety. The next she was forced out the door, gulping oxygen.

Terrified it would be her last.

TEXT MESSAGE: Send Anonymously 06:02 A.M.
Target acquired.

# Chapter Five

"What the hell happened?"

Levi grabbed the edge of a seat and hauled his disoriented body to its feet. He was alone in a passenger car full of black smoke. He dropped down to his knees coughing.

Smoke but no heat. Yet.

A glance at his watch verified he'd been unconscious for only a few minutes.

"Jo!" He couldn't see her or anything else.

All he could remember was his duffel hitting the back of his legs. He'd twisted to grab Jolene and thought he'd heard his name muffled under all the chaos. Then nothing. They had her. He didn't doubt that. He hadn't "tripped" into this passenger car.

Rubbing the back of his head, he mentally cursed his inability to protect Jolene—something that was becoming a habit. This time it might just be fatal.

*Get your butt out this door and find her!*

Easier said than done. The compartment door he'd been dragged through was jammed on the other side. Back of the train was no good—that's where the smoke came from. No duffel. No weapon.

*Trains. Emergency exit. Windows? Get 'em open. How? Hammer near the door.*

He couldn't see anything and shut his eyes to the burn-

ing pain of the smoke. He yanked his shirt over his head and secured it around his face. He took a deep breath and stood into the thicker blackness. Feeling with his hands along the wall, he remembered his quick walk-through of the train. A hammer and first aid kit were located near the door. He found the glass.

Hammer in hand, he dropped to his stomach to find some breathable air. He stayed as close to the floor for as long as he could, crawling to the window. Another deep breath, pounding on the window, cracking glass, still no air.

*Jo is in danger.*

*No one knows.*

Levi heard shouting, felt the compartment door slide. He attempted to get to his feet but someone hauled him from the passenger car. *Jo is in danger.* He had to get air and get moving.

Blessed oxygen filled his lungs. He gulped at the air and coughed, pushing a mask away from his face. He had no time.

"U.S. Marshal." He took in more air. "Secure the site. No one in or out." He got his eyes open, but focusing was another problem while they watered from the smoke. Dave and Max sucked down on their own oxygen. "Do you see her, Dave?"

"This is an open field, man. We can't round up everyone like cattle," stated by some form of local law enforcement.

Levi's eyes still burned. All he could make them focus on was a guy in uniform.

The older steward stretched taller and searched the crowd behind Levi. "She came off the train, wouldn't leave the door and told me you were still there. Forced me to go back in after you. We heard you pounding on the window."

Levi did some forcing of his own to get up. Where was

she? *If something happens to her on my watch...* He'd been out long enough for firefighters to arrive. They couldn't be in the middle of nowhere like he'd originally thought.

"Where are we?"

"Just north of Texarkana," Dave said. "The closest town is Hope, Arkansas."

Levi stuck out his hands and the EMT helped him to his unstable feet. He couldn't find Jolene alone. Dammit, he couldn't take two steps in a straight line without assistance.

"We need to get you to the hospital. You've got a nasty couple of cuts that need stitches, and you probably have a concussion."

Levi looked at the guy standing next to him. An EMT. Good.

"Not happening. I need a perimeter set, not only on any roads near here, but also on any major highways."

Levi kept walking, addressing the men who followed him, but searched for Jolene in the crowd. She could be wearing anything by now. He looked for that sassy hair-cut, but a short woman wasn't easily spotted in a crowd on a good day.

"Dave, get on your handset and check if anyone sees anything. No, wait. I think the guy who conked me was dressed as Amtrak." He turned to the firefighter. "Get me someone who can issue an APB."

A local cop or deputy walked into Levi's peripheral vision. "I'd like to see some ID before I let you take over this prank and it becomes a real train wreck."

"Prank? A woman's life is on the line. I need to find her...now."

"Those smoke bombs have already caused one fatality. I'm in charge unless you show me some ID and tell me what you were doing on that train."

*Fatality? Fatality! No! It couldn't be her.* The normal

adrenaline he'd experience may have been enough to kick him into gear, but the surge through his system was stimulated by pure fright.

He felt in his back pocket for his badge. "U.S. Marshal Levi Cooper out of Denver. I was escorting a…um, a person of interest. Now," he looked closely at the man's name, "Deputy Fordham, issue my APB. White female, twenty-five years old, five feet four inches, brown hair, emerald-green eyes. Last dressed in gray slacks and an Amtrak royal blue souvenir shirt four sizes too big."

"You got it. Not just green—emerald-green eyes. Right," he snickered and stepped toward the train, pulling his radio to his mouth.

"I'll spread the word," Dave said. He and Max took off quick and spry for men in their late fifties.

He turned to the EMT who treated the wound on his head every time Levi paused. "The deputy mentioned a fatality. Who and where?"

"She's at the rig."

"Take me."

The smoke escaping as the doors opened made it more difficult to see the crowd. But he could tell they were moving, thinning, walking or shifting to the road.

Lying on the ground next to the ambulance was one lone body bag waiting as if the rescuers had expected many more. Thank God it was just smoke bombs. It could have been a disaster.

His feet slowed. He needed to know. Had to kneel. Felt the damp from the morning grass seep through his jeans.

"Need some help?" the young fireman asked.

"I got it. Thanks." No matter how many bodies he'd seen, he'd never get used to looking at one that wasn't breathing. He gently unzipped the black plastic, dreading that this would be his last memory of Jolene.

"That her? Brown hair, average height, blue shirt. That your gal?"

The similarities struck him harder than whatever had hit him over the head. "No."

He resealed the bag and stood too fast, making his head spin. He shoved his hands through his hair, completely unable to think of what he should be doing. He had expected the woman to be Jolene. Until he'd seen the unknown woman's face, believing he'd find Jo alive hadn't seemed possible. This woman had either been mistaken for their target and then disposed or had been intended to be a distraction while they escaped.

"Where was she found?"

"Just inside the dining car."

*Distraction.*

"Whoever was on the train may have an accomplice who drove here." Levi turned in circles, taking in the countryside. One fire truck, two ambulances, numerous cars and trucks, people waiting to board the train.

"We were first on scene and none of the volunteers parked near here. They're all out on the main road."

"That's where she is." He broke into a run. Clear head or not, he wasn't going to lose Jo again. "Grab your gear. You're with me."

The EMT ran side by side with Levi. "Not sure how I can help you with anything, Marshal. I know I can help back at the train."

They reached the road, both sides of the single-lane pavement had deep culverts. "He didn't plan on a road like this. Maybe there's still time."

"Not so sure what you're talking about, sir."

"Look. There."

Every step connecting with the asphalt jarred a sharp pain in his head, but Levi didn't care. A car was half in

the ditch, looking like it was stuck on the incline, two men stared at the tires and scratched their heads. The long line of cars and trucks parked bumper-to-bumper had made it too difficult to steal.

His hand went to his hip. No weapon to draw, but no one else was in sight. "You know those guys?"

"Sure, that's Craig's car."

Levi crossed to the stuck vehicle. "U.S. Marshal, pop your trunk."

The man who was obviously Craig scratched his head again but walked to the driver's side. "I just called the sheriff. Stan noticed my car jacked at this angle. Looks like the guy got stuck and got scared off. Why's a marshal here?"

Could the man move any slower?

Levi, with the EMT next to him, waited to hear the latch click. His blood pounded through his body. This had to be it. Someone stealing a car, stuck, then looking for another vehicle. The two locals were lucky to still be alive.

Jo had to be here. *She has to be here.*

The trunk popped and blessed relief pushed the tension and pain straight from his body. Alive. They'd kept her alive. He staggered a couple of steps into the ditch out of the way.

"There's a body in here. Craig, go get the sheriff." The EMT reached through and immediately felt for a pulse, then gently shook her. "She's alive."

Craig and his friend ran toward the train.

Waiting for the firefighter to examine Jo drove him crazy. He couldn't think, let alone concentrate. He knew one thing—he wasn't leaving her. He'd depend on the locals to handle a search for her abductors.

"I think she's been drugged. Nothing I can do except transport."

"I've got her. Do whatever's necessary to get us out of here in three minutes."

"Yes, sir." The EMT jogged back the way they'd come, talking into his radio.

Levi scanned his line of sight one last time before sliding to the ground, car tire to his back and Jolene in his arms. When he'd heard "she's alive" his brain had jump-started.

The guy who had abducted her might be long gone, but he'd be back trying to find them soon. Levi's window of opportunity to keep her safe was shrinking.

"Don't you die on me, Jolene Atkins." He smoothed her hair, tucking it behind her ears, exposing a small scar that wasn't there the last time he'd seen her.

But he knew all about it from the monthly report he received. She'd fallen on a rollerblade date four months ago. Three stitches just in front of her right earlobe. He ran his thumb over the healed mark. "If I ever meet Darrell Taylor, I'll give him a strong lecture on what a good date should be. Never did tell your dad about the ER visit. Neither did you. Hang on, hon."

They hadn't killed her, just drugged her to get away without making a scene. When he caught them—and he would—they'd never harm her again.

# Chapter Six

Jolene stretched her arms, tried opening her eyes and quickly covered them. She wanted two aspirin before she moved too much. The pain in her head warranted stronger stuff than she had in her medicine cabinet. She rubbed her temples and swung her feet over the side of the bed, hitting a wall.

"Ow." Her eyes popped open. Her mind reset on what had happened the day before and the memory that was still clear in her mind. "Levi?"

"Hey, welcome back."

She heard his voice and soon a shirtless marshal emerged around the corner of a hotel bathroom.

"What happened?"

"You've been asleep for over twenty-four hours," he said, slipping into a T-shirt that lay across the back of a chair. "Bathroom's all yours."

*I lost an entire day?*

"The last thing I remember is the steward going into the train after you."

"Short summary version. The guy chasing us drugged you. I found you before he escaped, drove you to Dallas against doctor's orders and checked us into this hotel."

"And the guy who started the fire got away?"

One king-size bed. He'd slept there, the pillow next to her confirmed it.

"Just some major smoke bombs. And yeah, I stretched out on the bed. Don't get any ideas. I didn't let you take advantage of me."

Was her face that plain a road map for him to read? She popped out of bed, determined to get away from him. Her only choice was the bathroom he'd just vacated. She slid the door shut.

*No lock? What kind of a hotel didn't have a lock?*

"You are so full of yourself." She still wasn't clear of him since the steam was filled with his smell. She looked at the unmarked travel soap in the shower—his scent. Fresh, like it had just rained, clean.

Things were so different and yet she hadn't changed. The same person she was the day of the funeral stared back at her in the mirror. She felt hungry and well-rested even with the headache. No different than any other morning where she'd normally get dressed and go to work.

*Oh, my God.*

"These aren't my clothes."

"Yeah, well, the ones you had are still at the hospital," he said close to the door.

She gripped the counter by the sink. She couldn't speak, it was like she'd forgotten how. She was so completely mortified that he'd seen her naked.

"I sweet-talked a nurse into getting you dressed and sneaking you out at shift change." The words came through the door as if he were talking against the crack. "If anyone checks, it'll appear like you're still in the hospital with a new room. Might hold 'em off for a day."

"Oh." She leaned her head toward the sound of his voice. Was this a surge of disappointment and a sigh coming from her? *Ridiculous.*

"We got separated." She could open the door, but if she did she'd want him to hold her and she was terrified the kiss they'd shared had just been another distraction. "Someone tried to abduct me. Again."

"I know you don't feel like it at the moment, Jo, but I promise you're safe with me." His voice remained close to the door, softer, full of regret. "I'm not letting you out of my sight until I can turn you over to another marshal."

She shoved the door aside. "You're going to leave me?"

Panic. Pure and simple panic sat on her chest and she couldn't push it off. If she went into WITSEC she'd have another fictional existence. A new life, taking nothing with her. None of her friends, no Levi.

His hands were secure on her shoulders. Firm, but not holding her in place…just close enough to make her want more.

"It's the only way and what your father wanted."

"*I* don't want that life." She shoved past him and the temptation to have his arms wrap tighter around her. "I don't believe that's what my father intended. He convinced me to leave Boulder. He wanted me to have a life, not constantly be looking over my shoulder like he had done for twenty years."

"That's not what his letter said."

"His letter said I needed protection *if* I remembered. Well, I haven't remembered. I don't want to remember!"

*Concentrate on the problem, not the man. Think.* She moved to the window overlooking the outskirts of Dallas.

"Take it easy." When he moved toward her, she held her finger up and he stopped in his tracks. "In case you've forgotten, I nearly got you killed twice. I can't do this alone."

"Isn't there a way to just catch these guys and be done with it?"

"Whatever your dad found stirred up this hornet's nest.

Our best bet is to find it and turn it over to the DoJ. Then they can reopen the case."

"We don't know what *it* even is. And afterward, I'll be stuck wherever. Doing whatever. Lying forever."

"You'll be alive."

She didn't want to admit he was her only choice. She hated that phrase. Her dad had repeated "we have no choice" with each slumber party invitation he refused to let her accept. Her first date was verified and checked out by the Marshals Service. If her dad hadn't been a chaperone at the senior prom, there might have been someone undercover there, too. Maybe there had been. She didn't know anything anymore.

The Marshals Service had kept its end of the bargain with her mother. WITSEC had protected them even though her mother had been the actual witness.

It didn't matter. They had to catch the one person responsible for killing her parents. If they didn't, she would never have a real life. Bottom line—she didn't want to live like her father and she would never share that life with anyone she loved. Keeping that secret or dragging someone into that situation wouldn't be fair.

She moved, defeated, to the edge of the bed and there he was directly in front of her again.

"What do you remember?" He raised a finger to stop her protest. "Just talk to me. Don't try. Start with why you think your family was in protective custody."

"Dad testified against one of the men who murdered my mother. The guy was stabbed while in a federal penitentiary and died. But the Department of Justice was never able to connect his actions to the person my mom was supposed to testify against."

"Accurate so far. What do you remember about the day of the murder?"

"Nothing much. Men arguing with my mother. I think she yelled at my dad." The headache was worse. She needed aspirin. "It's more impressions than words or actual memories."

"That's okay. You said you remembered hiding in your toy box. Why?"

"That's where I thought they found me." She didn't like the look on his face. "You've given me that look before. The same one that says I'm on the right track, but the wrong train."

"Let's not talk about trains," he said, rubbing his head and scratching around a small bandage.

"Are you hurt?"

"The bastard hit me over the head. Gave me six stitches." He put his hand on her knee as he sat next to her, but quickly pulled it back when she jerked.

"Oh, my God."

"I'm okay. Nothing serious. And I didn't mean to scare you."

"Not that. I just remembered." She faced him, finally excited she had something new to share. "It happened on the train, with all the smoke and noise I couldn't tell you."

"Go ahead, don't force it."

"Close to the murder, I'm not certain what day it was, but I remember hurting my finger on the upstairs railing. For some reason, some of the nails— What are they, the little tiny ones?"

"Finishing nails."

"That's right."

Levi watched as her words faded and she was taken back twenty years. He wanted to ask a dozen questions, but knew to keep his mouth shut. Her words had to come at their own pace.

"I hurt my finger and went to my mother so she could

fix it. I couldn't help seeing that someone was in the kitchen with her. I think it was one of her clients and a secretary. They were all arguing. My mother looked really worried."

The memories were coming back a lot faster than he'd anticipated. "Do you remember anything about the day? Was it sunny? Dark? Raining?"

"I remember a lot of rainbows."

"There were crystals hanging in the window. They must have caught the light and shot prisms through the room. So it was during the afternoon."

"How do you know about the crystals?"

"Photos from the scene. Layout of the house."

"So that would explain the 'rainbow man' from my dreams."

*A rainbow man?* She'd been holding out on him a lot more than he'd thought.

"Can you picture him?"

She shook her head and flattened her lips. "No."

In his experience, when witnesses were compelled to remember, they either filled in the gaps with wrong information or shut down. Changing the subject should get her relaxed without forcing the issue. "Why was your mom worried?"

"I don't know, but she was. She had the dish towel drying dishes. Dad said she only cleaned the kitchen when she was worried. She'd cleaned every day for a week. I didn't think of that before."

She smiled, obviously excited about her discovery. If only she knew how much she looked like the photo of her mother. It must have been hard for Joseph to watch her grow up without thinking of his wife every day.

"Why do you think it was unusual to clean the kitchen? Everybody does it."

"We had a part-time maid, someone who helped my mother."

*That wasn't in the reports.* How many other people had been in the house who aren't in the freakin' report? "So she didn't live with you or have a key to the house?"

"I don't think so. LuLu watched me when I was sick. And allowed me to play in the downstairs living room while she dusted. She'd let me sit on top of the vacuum and would push me around. I loved staying home from daycare."

"Do you remember LuLu's real name?"

She thought a moment, cupping both her cheeks with her slender, delicate fingers. Physically growing more tense with each glance around the room. "I can't. It's all blurring together. I don't know what's real and what's a dream."

"Time to stop." He took her hands from her face, relieved she let him touch her without jumping out of her skin. "Don't force it."

"Why not try? I've remembered more in the last ten minutes than twenty years."

"Your dad was right. Your memory has been coming back with a vengeance. You just didn't realize it."

"If you don't want me to talk, then *you* should. Why didn't you mention you'd seen the file on my mother?"

"I see the case file on all my witnesses."

"Okay then, spill."

"I'm not going to tell you what I know." He wanted to. Wanted to be completely honest for once. "Don't read any secretiveness into it, either. If I told you, it may change what you actually remember. But I can say that there was no mention of a part-time maid in any reports. She would have been a good person to interrogate at the time of the murder."

"Dad would have mentioned her."

"Then we assume her information has been removed from the files," he said, looking a bit worried for once. "Or she's there and not listed as having access to the house."

"So where do we start?"

"You get showered and dressed. Then we go visit your old house." He propped his back against the headboard. "I'm not leaving you alone. I'm sticking to you like leather seats on a hot humid day. No buts or arguing. Get used to it."

Her cute little dimpled jaw fell open with a little puff of astonishment, but she quickly recovered and retreated to the bath. He heard the water spray and needed to close his eyes. He'd driven throughout the night. Until they identified her mother's client, the mysterious housekeeper and this *Rainbow Man*, he'd be sleeping with one eye open.

He'd purchased a burner cell to update his office on the train fiasco and ask a pal for a favor. Still hadn't made the call yet. Sherry would be furious and think he was out of his mind.

If she hadn't thought he was nuts for helping Jo before, she would when he told her that his non-witness was on the verge of identifying a murderer who looked like a *Rainbow Man*.

"IT SHOULD JUST be a couple of more blocks. We're going to drive by once to see if we can spot anyone watching the house."

Levi spoke in his natural, calming manner. Seemingly unconcerned that Jolene was about to enter her childhood home. A place she'd only allowed herself to remember with happy childlike impressions.

But she saw his eyes, searching the mirror, the streets, watching those walking by just a little longer than normal. His voice might be soothing, but his body spoke a differ-

ent language. Defensive, ready to strike, protective, fingers tight on the steering wheel, ready to race the car and get them out of there in an instant. She knew he'd readied his gun at the hotel, verified how many bullets he had one last time before placing it in his holster.

So many of the things she'd wondered about over the past four years made sense now. She loved the curiosity in his eyes that had seemed to be constantly searching and seeking. His toned body came to mind without thinking. Who wouldn't admire that? She'd mentioned it to her father once and he'd said Levi had a great gym membership.

It was hard to remember the "friendship" between her dad and the "new kid at work" hadn't been real. It seemed very sincere at the numerous dinners Levi had joined. None of that mattered. Her father was just a case number to Marshal Cooper. She was an obligation and Levi felt guilty for not keeping her safe. He sat next to her because of a promise to her father. And she let him because she needed his assistance.

Nothing more.

She should remember their being together had nothing to do with feelings or friendship. No matter how many kisses they shared, he'd made it very clear two years ago that nothing else could happen between them. In the many hours they'd spent together during the past two days, there had been no attempt to assure her things were different.

There wasn't a future between them.

Period.

Jolene's insides were in knots. The tension wrenching her muscles caused an achy tightness like she'd just run a half marathon. She loved running, but never experienced this sick feeling of dread.

Maybe it was just the part she was to play. She wasn't sure she could pull it off, but Levi had insisted that the

owner not know her true association with the house. Her dad always had a plan. And a backup. "Always be prepared for the first to fail," he used to say. So flying by the seat of her pants was not only new, it just felt...wrong.

"What do you expect to happen? What am I supposed to do?"

Levi moved as if he was going to hold her hand, but she quickly lifted hers to rub the back of her neck. The close proximity of him was hard enough to control. Touching was out of the question. He might insist on sharing a room, but he was definitely pushing the two chairs together and not sleeping in her bed. All six-plus feet of him.

"You aren't supposed to do anything." He used the hand originally headed her direction to push that stray curl off his forehead. "Just see if you remember anything. Don't try too hard, just let it happen."

"And how is my character supposed to act?"

"I think you could act as normal and natural as you always do."

She had her doubts about that last statement. They turned onto the street where she'd lived, he'd given her the address, she could see the house numbers, knew when they passed it. Nothing happened.

No recognition. No feeling. No spark of emotion.

"It's a pretty little house," she said, turning in her seat to stare longer, trying hard to remember. "Do they know we're coming?"

Levi's hand covered hers and she snapped around, yanking her hand back to her lap. The warmth lingered longer than she wanted to admit.

"What do you remember about your mother?"

"Impressions. Dark hair, tall, she spoke in whispers. LuLu was actually the one who took me to the park. I remember her catching me at the end of the slide or darting

under my swing as she pushed me high in the sky. Childish memories that abruptly stop. It's like another life."

"Did you ever overhear her talk about cases?"

"Cases? What do you mean?"

He opened his mouth, then flattened his lips and scratched his freshly shaven chin. The car was stopped at an intersection. He took another quick look around and then twisted in his seat to look at her. "Your mother was a defense attorney with some very high-powered clients."

"I had no idea. I've spent my entire life with my father who avoided the subject of my mother. No matter how many times I asked, he never spoke of her. Ever."

If she had to describe Levi's actions, she'd say the line of questioning made him extremely uncomfortable. He was practically squirming. She'd never seen him this indecisive. He hesitated, clearly struggling with how to answer.

"Not to you, but he did talk about her."

"Really, Levi. You're just telling me now?" She watched him return to driving the car. "Your timing needs a lot of work."

"Yeah, I know."

"You're not going to tell me anything else though. Are you?" Did she see a moment of sadness cross his expression before he shook his head?

"I will. I just don't think it's a good idea before you remember."

"And if I never do?"

"You already are, Jolene. You ready to do this?"

They were parked in front of the house.

"No, but that doesn't matter, does it?"

She got out without looking at him again. If she saw one second of remorse or hesitation, she'd tell him to take her back to the hotel.

A variety of roses were planted on either side of the

walk and house. A virtual rainbow of colors side by side. *Rainbows.* She couldn't take another step. Levi had a hand at her back, gently encouraging her with a slight pressure to move forward.

"You can do this, Jo. I'm right here. We're just going to knock on the door. Okay?"

She must have nodded her head. They moved. He knocked. He talked, showed his badge. They moved.

One little step at a time. That's all she could accomplish. She stared at her feet. Actually being here was a lot harder than she'd anticipated. Much harder to look up and not recognize anything except the stair rail.

*Nails. Rainbows. Blood.*

"Mama."

# Chapter Seven

"Hey, hon, do you need to sit? You're sort of swaying on your feet." The bleached blonde, gum-smacking Mrs. Colter stuck a glass of water as far away from herself as possible. Nowhere near Jolene.

Levi waved off the drink and trapped Jo's waist tighter to his side—if that were possible.

"I'm fine." Jolene pushed at his hands.

The moment was gone. She stood straight and looked at him as if he were the one in a trance or about to faint.

"You sure you're okay?" He released his life-saving grip, skimming his hand down the side of her cool arm and latching onto her ice-cold fingers. "You were kind of sleepwalking for a minute."

"So you're a real psychic? You didn't see a ghost or anything, did you?" Mrs. Colter asked.

"No, nothing like that. I'm sorry, were we introduced?"

Jo seemed fine answering. Like nothing had happened. Did she have a clue she'd been talking out loud? *Nails. Rainbows. Blood.* She seemed to have remembered something the moment she stepped onto the sidewalk. He'd have to wait to find out exactly what, since the new owner of the house was completely enthralled with their cover story about trying to solve a twenty-year-old murder.

"Oh, I'm Sadie Colter and I've been hoping to see a

ghost in this house since the night I moved in fourteen years ago, you know? No luck for me though."

"You sure you're okay?" he asked after seeing how colorless Jo's cheeks were.

She completely ignored him, took the water and politely shook Mrs. Colter's hand. "Annabel Drummond. Thank you for allowing me in your home today. As I told the marshal, I've been having dreams about the unsolved crime that took place here."

"You mean the triple homicide?" the older woman asked. "Or the other thing?"

*Don't fall apart, Jo.*

She threw her shoulders back. "Could you tell us what you know about both?"

*Asked like a pro.*

"Sure, come on into the living room," Mrs. Colter said and led the way.

Levi leaned close to Jo and whispered, "You're doing great." His praise was met with a look that told him just what he could do with it.

"You know, I'm not exactly sure what I expected a psychic to be like, but you aren't exactly what I had pictured." Mrs. Colter laughed, nervously smoothing her tight red pants that matched her brightly painted toes.

"Lots of people say that." Jo sat on the edge of a denim-covered chair, one of the few places free of cat fur.

Standing was a better option for him. He didn't need to watch the conversation, and observing the street traffic or anything unusual was a priority to keep Jo safe. So he listened, keeping the women's reflections in the windowpanes.

"Well, I suppose you know all about the attorney who was murdered here. From the research I did, I'm almost an expert, you know?" Mrs. Colter paused only long enough

to fill her lungs. "Anyway, she was a big to-do attorney working for the wrong people. That will always come back to bite you in the butt, darlin'. Never work for the wrong people. Has there been any new development I don't know about?"

"I can't say. Please continue, Mrs. Colter." Jolene didn't flinch or move at all. She listened.

No movement on the street, not even a postman.

"Oh honey, call me Sadie, everybody does. Anyway, absolutely no one knows for certain what she did to get herself killed. But you know what, no matter if she deserved it or not, her husband and little girl didn't deserve it. No sir-reedee. That little girl was only five years old. Just five short years old. You pickin' up on something again, hon?"

Levi caught Jo before she marched from the room, swinging her around to face him. "What's wrong?"

"I can't do this," she whispered with a clenched jaw.

"Oh, do you need to be alone to work your magic?" Mrs. Colter asked.

"No, she's fine." He was certain she'd bolt if he let go of her elbow. He lowered his voice. "I've got you."

Jo's look of complete disbelief shot through his heart. She really didn't believe he'd protect her. And he couldn't— at least not from the lost memories she didn't want to accept.

"Anyway." Mrs. Colter didn't let Jo's attempt to leave slow her storytelling. "From what I found out, all three were professionally gunned down in the kitchen. Such a lovely room, too, you know? It's full of sunlight all the time."

Elaine Frasier had been stabbed, but he didn't correct her.

"And the second incident you mentioned?" Jolene asked, unsuccessfully attempting to slip from his grasp.

"Why, the next owner, Gerald Major, you know? He

bought the house for practically nothing, you know? And then it was up for sale again. He was murdered in downtown Dallas not three years later."

"Why did *you* buy the house, Mrs. Colter?" Jo asked with a hesitant voice.

"I thought for certain it would be haunted. And it was dirt-cheap, you know? Easy to convince Eugene to make the deal."

"Can we see the rest of the rooms? Do you mind if Annabel wanders alone?"

"Oh, not at all. I'll wait here keeping my fingers crossed she can sense some paranormal activity, you know?"

Jolene's look was either dread or simply disbelief that he expected her to explore on her own. But she quickly left him with Mrs. Colter, only pausing a second before stepping on the bottom stair. He watched until she disappeared from view.

Mrs. Colter popped her gum mid-sentence, forcing him to listen to her once again. "I've always been interested in ghosts, ever since I seen that movie *Poltergeist,* you know?"

He checked the street perimeter. His hand went to his weapon, but there was nothing there. "Is your block normally this quiet?"

"Yeah, even after twenty years and a couple of new paint jobs, most people avoid it."

"I'm curious, were all the flowers here before?"

"Well, a lot of them died over the years. But I've had the lawn guy replace them, keeping them exactly the same. It sort of looks like a rainbow, you know?"

*Again with the rainbows.*

Levi's job depended on precision planning and good execution. He didn't need to trust his instincts. He'd never experienced the tiny hairs on the back of his neck prick-

ling at a sign of danger. But if he had to describe why his gut felt tangled and the weird feeling of something crawling up his spine—that just might be it.

Something was off. A bad vibe.

He moved to the doorway and caught sight of Jo on the upstairs landing. Walking from door to door, swaying as if she were unsteady on her feet. She glanced in, then moved on to the next room.

He could hear his blood thumping in his ears in the split second between her swaying and catching herself on the door frame. He took the first stairs two at a time, then slowed and made as little noise as possible. If she were remembering, he didn't want to yank her away.

"Y'all doin' okay?" Mrs. Colter said from where he'd stood moments before.

Jo turned, met his eyes and dropped her shoulders with a heavy sigh. "I'm fine. I'm afraid I haven't remem—received any otherworldly messages." She pivoted and headed down the stairs. "Mrs. Colter, is there anything left from the victims? Anything associated with…rainbows?"

He was one step behind Jo.

"Oh. My. God. So you did pick up on something."

Mrs. Colter shuffled across the tile floor, looking like she wanted to run, but unable to pick up her strapless sandals. He hated noticing everything about her. He was in that mode, though. Searching for potential threats was what he was good at. Standing on the sidelines without a plan wasn't.

As much as he wanted to follow through on her memories, he couldn't continue to make mistakes with Jo's life. Being here was a mistake. He led her to the bottom of the stairs.

"I'm…I'm not sure. I just keep seeing rainbows."

Jolene's voice went all breathy again. She latched onto Levi's forearm with a death grip.

"There's this old birdhouse that fell apart ages ago," said Mrs. Colter. "I wouldn't let Eugene throw it out. He put the pieces in the shed."

"Can you take us to it?" Levi asked, delaying their departure against his better judgment.

"Sure, but don't you want to see what was stuck inside?"

"Was it something like a dog?"

"Oh, my God. You're for real." She ran up the stairs.

"I can't do this anymore." Jo turned her face into his chest.

He guided her back to the chair. Instead of sitting, she looked up, tears pooling and enhancing the green sparkles in her eyes. He wrapped his arms around her slender body. The urge to walk away before the owner returned was so great he had to pull his foot back a step.

Jo didn't deserve this sadness, but she'd strangle him if it were all for nothing.

"I don't understand why Joseph put this on your shoulders to finish," he said, whispering into her ear. "He must have had his reasons, but I know that you were the *only* thing important to him. The *only* thing he loved."

"It was easier to believe that yesterday. Right now, I feel like a pawn in his game of revenge." She patted his chest, leaning away. "I don't know why the image of a carved wooden dog popped into my head. I can't remember Mama putting it inside a birdhouse."

"Maybe she didn't." When was he supposed to hand her the statue in his duffel? Joseph's instructions wrapped around the dog by a rubber band, said he'd know when it was right. Now there was a second one?

"Who then?"

Levi released her and Jolene collapsed on the edge of the

loveseat, waiting to confront one of her mother's favorite gifts. She could remember it was very special. She'd gotten in trouble on more than one occasion for touching it and…

"It has a hidey space. That's what Dad called it. I don't remember what to do, but somehow the bottom pivots open."

"We can't let—" He abruptly stopped when the home-owner appeared in the door. "Mrs. Colter, we're fortunate you kept this piece of evidence."

"I tried to give it to the police when we found it, but they said the case was closed. I didn't think that the limitations thingy ever expired on murder, you know?"

Why wouldn't they have taken it or called her mother's murder case 'closed'? Unless the Marshals Service wanted it closed due to her father's WITSEC status. Yet another question.

Levi met the excited woman at the doorway and blocked her from Jolene's sight. "May I?"

Whatever she handed him, he put straight into his jacket pocket.

"No tellin' how long it had been there. The police said they didn't think it had anything to do with either mur-der, but I already had it in the bag. It's filthy, but just like I found it."

There was a clear picture in her mind of a brown-stained cocker spaniel. She knew they couldn't open it here and didn't need to see the little statue. The image of a dark-haired woman taking it from her hands and placing it on a high shelf out of a five-year-old's reach was as clear as any photograph.

"Can we see the backyard?" she asked before thinking it through. She didn't want to see the broken birdhouse. In fact, she was frightened out of her skin. She'd come this far, though.

Pawn or loving daughter, she'd play her part. There was no other choice if she wanted her life back.

Levi looked at her as if she was crazy for asking. She didn't want to go out there. Staying another minute in that house pretending to be a psychic wasn't the perfect choice, either. But how could she make him understand? She was *never* coming back to this place again. Ever.

Somehow Sadie Colter sensed that quiet was needed or warranted. Or Jo had just learned to block out the woman's very southern drawl. Either thing worked as they passed by the kitchen. Jolene kept her head turned to the opposite wall so she wouldn't see any part of it. Not yet. She knew it was coming, but if the dreams mixed with reality again, she wanted it to be the last thing that happened.

Mrs. Colter remained quiet, and once in the background, she raised her finger pointing toward a well-kept building in the far corner of the yard. The entire effect of archways, vines and flowers was magical. The trees were tall, strong oaks. One branch had a rope swing. The rope and wood were new, obviously not from the time she'd lived in the house, but she remembered them.

And LuLu.

A young blonde in her early twenties. Her eyes went from the swing to Mrs. Colter. It couldn't be. But the feeling of recognition swept over her like a warm, relaxing shower. She watched Sadie Colter retreat into the kitchen.

"Annabel," Levi called to her. "This birdhouse must have been huge. You'll have to come inside to get a look at the pieces. You sure you're up for this?"

"Yes. I'm not coming back here a second time."

He accepted her statement in stride, and opened the door to a very well organized workshop and storage area.

"Before we go any further..." She hadn't asked for details before they'd arrived, but the image of LuLu was

quickly becoming Sadie Colter in her mind. "Is she real? You've checked her out, right?"

"Who? Mrs. Colter? My contact at the Service said she bought the house in an estate auction. I assumed it was the estate of your family, not another murder victim. We'll check into that later. Let's speed things up, been here way too long."

"I agree. I just need to see the kitchen after this and—"

"A look at the birdhouse and then we're out of here. It's almost sick how she's kept everything the same. This woman is certifiably weird." Levi turned his back to Jo and stood at the entrance. He was just behind the door, out of sight to anyone who might threaten them.

He was trying so hard to protect her. She knew that. This situation wasn't his fault. He blamed himself for leading her mother's client to the funeral and thought she blamed him. The truth was she was glad he'd come.

Just knowing he'd been on the hill behind her brought her comfort. Someone who knew her dad. Someone to share the grief other than the couple of her mother's distant relations who had attended out of curiosity. She hadn't been allowed to tell them it was her father in the casket.

The beautiful garden looked better than she remembered from her childhood. Her father had taken so much time planting the flowers into half circles. He'd built the flowerbeds himself. She remembered the piles and piles of dirt and the countless times he'd pushed her tricycle over the top.

Her head hurt with all the memories rushing in. She dabbed at her cheeks, hiding the tears from Levi. She remembered things so vividly she was scared to go into the kitchen or see the birdhouse.

But she had to hold it together and get through this.

"Where did you see the pieces?"

He didn't need to point or answer. As soon as she'd asked, the faded paint caught her attention.

Weathered boards stacked neatly at the back of the work table blended into the wood until she noticed the design she'd help create. Touching the washed-out colors on the rainbow took as much courage as seeing her father prepared for his burial.

The flying birds and butterflies made her heart skip a beat. Her daddy had built the birdhouse in this very room. He used the tools that still hung on the wall, now covered with layers of rust. He'd held her hand steady as they'd painted each arch of color, drawn the outline of each bird she'd help obscure by blobbing on the blue paint.

Her fingers slid over the battered spot of yellow she'd added on her own. It represented the giant bird on TV. Her father had been surprised, but laughed so hard his eyes watered. She'd been so proud to make him happy.

"I miss you so much, Daddy."

"Come on, Jo. We've got to go." Levi took her hand and led her to the door.

"But…what about the kitchen?"

"There's no time. This feels… For someone so curious, our hostess has been strangely absent. Something's not right."

"It's that woman."

He stopped and looked at her. "What do you mean?"

"I know this sounds off the wall, but I think she's LuLu."

"Damn it, Jolene, why didn't you tell me? How do we get out of here?" He spun in a three-sixty, getting his bearings and pulled his gun. "Driveway's that way."

He yanked her through the wooden gate just in time to see two men walk around the corner of the house, guns drawn. The longer barrels were equipped with silencers.

"Run, Jo. And don't look back."

"You promised you wouldn't leave me alone. I'm keeping you to that." She grabbed his belt loop under his jacket.

"Don't argue with me about this." He broke free from her hold. "I can't protect you unless you leave first. I'm right behind you. Now go."

He didn't point out a direction, but there seemed to be only one available—a small open space between the shed and fence. Odd things were piled on top of each other. She climbed them, hearing a couple of shots from Levi's gun. She hopped over the fence, using a cross piece to help her down onto the grass.

The house backed up to some sort of wooded area. Each direction looked exactly the same—uncut grass and trees. More gunfire. She heard the wood splinter as the *silenced* bullets hit the shed. She ran. Hard. Fast. Slipping in the new shoes they'd bought earlier that day.

"Keep running. Don't look back."

She did, worried he wasn't behind her. She darted behind a tree to catch her breath.

Circle back to the car? She could see another house ahead of them. Which way was the best choice? Her heart was in her throat and her mind raced faster than she could comprehend the information it released.

"Which way?"

"Right!" Levi yelled from just behind her. He closed the distance, passed her and continued left toward another fence. She ran next to him along the fence until they came to another yard and slipped between the houses, around a corner and onto a porch.

He pressed his back to her chest, flattening them against the brick of the house. Levi didn't speak. He didn't have to. She could feel his heart pounding through his shirt. Feel his muscles tensed under her hands.

Thinking was more difficult while hiding from men attempting to kill you. She wanted to gulp air. Shout. Beat down the door to one of these homes. Get help. Call for the police. She didn't do any of those things.

"Let's go," Levi commanded. He'd inched away from her, looking back the way they'd come, slipping his hand to her hip, keeping her in place.

"I've got to rest." After the scorching her lungs had taken with the smoke the previous day, breathing was hard work.

"Get moving, Jolene. You run farther than this every day."

She did jog almost every morning, but... "How do you know I run?"

# Chapter Eight

"We've got to get moving. They're right on our tails."

He'd screwed up. First by assuming the men at the train wouldn't find them this quickly, and second by letting it slip he'd kept tabs on Jolene while she was in Georgia. He'd never intended to inform Jo her father had asked him to make certain she was safe after she'd moved away. By the time he'd been asked by Joseph, he'd already called in a couple of favors from friends assigned in the area to check up on Jolene.

Yeah, he knew she ran every morning. He also knew why. Freedom. Her father had never allowed it. As soon as she'd moved to Georgia, she'd begun jogging outdoors.

It drove him insane to think about her in the open, unprotected. Sort of like now. He had never told Joseph.

The buzz acted like an electric shock to Levi. He spun around on the confined porch. His brain delayed recognition of the sound until he saw Jolene's face. She'd pressed the doorbell. Deliberately.

It was a big risk to holster their only defense, but he put the gun away and pulled his badge.

"Can I help you?" an older woman asked as she cracked the door open.

Still no one rounding the corner, no running footsteps, no yelling, no cars. He pressed his ID to the screen. "U.S.

Marshal Cooper, ma'am. May we come inside? This is an emergency."

The woman placed her glasses on her nose, squinted and disappeared. The door swung open and Jolene went inside. Levi took another look around the corner of the house—still nothing.

They'd lost them? Too easy. *Nothing was that easy.*

"I understand you're a bit afraid right now, ma'am," Jo reassured her, "but I think we should ask Marshal Cooper if he wants the police called."

"Rebecca Mossing, dear. As old as I am, I still shudder at being referred to as ma'am."

Levi had missed the first part of the conversation, but he caught up to speed quick enough. And as much as he didn't want the Plano PD involved, there wasn't a way to avoid it.

"Feel free, ma'am. Let them know shots were fired at 1936 Briarcreek Lane." Now he'd endangered a grandmother. One glance around the room let him know she had four grandchildren—their pictures were everywhere.

"Oh, my, guns?"

"If you'd like me to speak with them, just point me to the phone."

The silver-haired woman held her hand in the air. "No, no. I did away with the land line a couple of years ago. I'm all digital, but I left my cell in the car."

"I don't want to put you in harm's way—"

"I'll be fine. The garage is connected to the kitchen. The back door's already secure. Throw the dead bolt on the front, Marshal, and catch your breath. I'll be right back."

"Jo, can you get the door and see if our friends are following from the window?" Levi followed the granny from the room. She left the door open behind her, dug in a purse she grabbed from the front seat and pressed but-

tons. She nodded and told the emergency operator her name and address.

He left their hostess to check on the kitchen door. No fence, no dog, no cover. Easy to see if someone followed them through the woods.

"She's a surprise," Jo said, letting the front curtains fall back into place.

"That was a gutsy move, ringing the bell. You should have asked." As he approached, Jo stepped aside, avoiding contact as he took his place beside her. Safer for her on an interior wall. From his vantage point he could keep watch on both the front of the house and the backyard.

Still nothing.

"I know you're in charge, *Marshal* Cooper. You don't have to remind me at every turn."

"Come on, Jo, don't be this way."

"The police said there's an officer on his way and that you should stay put." Mrs. Mossing sat on the small sofa. "Here's my cell if you need to call anyone."

"Thanks for your help, Mrs. Mossing," Jolene said without a hint of the sarcasm she'd been using with him.

"Not a problem, dear. Don't hesitate." She handed Jolene the phone. "I have unlimited air time."

Jo held the phone. He wasn't worried she'd use it. Who would she call? He continued watching through the blinds for any sign they'd been followed or the police to show.

"Should I stay here or go sit in my bedroom anxiously awaiting my interview with the police?" Rebecca Mossing asked. "I assume you aren't going to tell me why someone was firing at you. It seems that house really is cursed."

"You know about the murders?" Jo asked.

"I've lived here a long time, dear. Robert Frasier de-

signed my yard. Their little girl was truly adorable. They loved her so much. All those pretty dresses she wore."

"You knew them? The...the Frasiers?"

"Oh, yes." Mrs. Mossing patted Jo's knee. "Robert was a wonderful landscaper. And these houses were so bleak back then. He took care of most of the homes in this edition. Wonderful man, so sad. The landscaping around here just hasn't been the same."

This discussion was dangerous ground. What if Mrs. Mossing recognized Jo, or should he say Emaline, all grown up? The resemblance to her mother was uncanny. If Jo had four more inches, she could have been a clone. How could he stop her from pursuing information about her parents?

"When Robert married a Dallas attorney, I knew several divorced women who were more than a little surprised and so very disappointed."

Jolene had done so well all day, he hated to risk anything else and needed to get her out of here. The mention of her father brought a soft smile to her face and relaxed her shoulders.

Cop sirens.

"Our ride's here," he said.

"What should I tell the police?" their hostess asked.

"The truth, Mrs. Mossing. Just the truth. We appreciate your help, ma'am." Jo joined him at the door. "Wait here. I'll be back to get you. If things go wrong..."

"They won't."

"Still playing the psychic?" He tried to make her smile at him. No luck.

Levi met the car at the curb, badge in hand, jacket open showing his weapon, waving off the officer's potential questions. "Your ID?" The officer complied. "I have a

witness that needs immediate transportation no questions asked, no radio. Do you have a vest?"

Levi had spent time serving warrants and transporting criminals. After moving to WITSEC he'd taken his share of witnesses into protective custody—cooperating or against their will, alone or with a partner. This ride was their only way out. He had no choice and knew whoever was after Jolene, still watched.

Jo waited with Mrs. Mossing at the door. He headed back with the vest and the women hugged. Jo nodded in agreement of something.

"What was that about?" he asked.

"She wished me luck. I think we need it."

He had a feeling that wasn't all the grandmother had said.

With the help of the officer, Jolene was transferred to a local police department. In silence. Levi admired her. No matter how he strived to treat her just like another witness, it wasn't going to happen. He appreciated her calm, her restraint, her trust that he knew what he was doing.

A crappy feeling churned in the pit of his stomach. Doubt in his ability, his judgment. What made him think he could handle the organization that took out Jo's parents alone?

Didn't matter. They were here. It was happening. Time to focus on protecting his witness. Thirty minutes later, there had been limited explanations and agreement to use an unmarked car to return to their hotel.

"Phone call." The sergeant who'd been helping them pointed toward a room. "You can use this office."

Levi knew who was on the phone. Any good cop would have checked out his credentials and called Denver. He'd wanted to avoid getting his butt chewed in front of Jo, hoping to make the call when it wasn't necessary to keep

her directly next to him. They both entered the room and shut the door.

Jo had said three words: coffee, cream and please. That's it. Now she sat next to the phone.

"Cooper."

"Who the hell do you think you are? I want explanations for abusing your status as a United States Marshal." Sherry spoke loud enough to be heard without a speaker. There wasn't a way to turn down the volume or walk away from the extension.

"I identified myself in Texarkana and helped with the search. Nothing more."

"Don't insult my intelligence. A train was set on fire and you absconded with a victim, crossing state lines. You're currently in Dallas working a twenty-year-old murder. Shots have been fired."

"You knew I was escorting Jolene—"

"You aren't escorting a witness, Cooper. There. Is. No. Witness. Period. Did you hear me that time?"

"Yes, ma'am. Loud and clear."

*As could Jolene.*

"You'll be lucky if you can keep your job over this incident. How long have you been having an affair with her?"

"You checked my files?"

"Of course we checked your files. I have a rogue marshal flashing his badge around in two different states. *Of course* I gave the order. All the *favors* you've asked from fellow marshals in the Atlanta area, switching with others to pull duty in the area yourself. This goes way beyond stalking, Cooper."

The shocked expression on Jo's face verified that she'd heard, too.

"If you found the files, then you know there was no af-

fair. I was watching my witness. Joseph Atkins knew his daughter would be in danger. I have his statements—"

"Atkins's death is an unfortunate accident. He and his family are no longer the responsibility of the Marshals Service."

"I led the people trying to kill her straight to the funeral. Hell, I practically bought their plane tickets."

"Don't push this any further, Levi. Walk away."

"Not happening. I gave my word."

"Then I have no choice. You're officially suspended."

"Well that didn't go as planned," Levi said, coming through the hotel door just behind her.

Jolene toed her shoes off, leaving each directly in Levi's path and totally not caring. *Let him trip.* She hadn't spoken. Not a word. She hadn't known what to say at the police station. Since the phone call from Levi's supervisor suspending him, she hadn't been capable of forming a coherent sentence.

How could she be furious, terrified, mortified and betrayed all at the same time? The desire to let loose a bloodcurdling scream of frustration had never been as strong as it was finding out he'd been spying on her.

"You ready to talk?" he asked. He'd been silent and hopefully a little embarrassed.

Where did she begin? Levi was certain to have a logical explanation. She looked through the curtains, careful to keep her body next to the wall instead of the glass like her father had taught her. Leaving the long, gold drape in place, she watched rush hour traffic on the nearby highway. Car after car sped forward only to stop again several yards ahead.

Sort of like her life. Full of starts and stops and unexpected turns. Just when she thought she was moving

forward, something happened to push her in a different direction. Last week she was sitting behind a desk with an unexciting career in her future. Today…being shot at by unknown murderers—someone attempting to discover a secret that had died with her mother.

And then there was Levi. She'd just begun to trust him again. Why had he lied to her? Again. Could she forgive him for fulfilling a promise to her father?

*Maybe, but not right this second.*

The kiss two years ago had been a distraction. The kiss on the train—another distraction. It must have been. He'd made it very clear that he couldn't become involved with a witness. And he considered her a witness. He'd made *that* very clear to his supervisor.

"I'd rather talk about what happened at the house," she finally admitted.

"We probably shouldn't ignore what you think happened over the past two years."

"What I *think* happened?" A surge of fury raced through her, causing her fingers to curl into fists. "There's a lot of things you need to explain, but let's see if what I *think* happened is correct."

"Okay."

"My father wanted to investigate my mother's death so he lied to me about the danger to his life. He encouraged me to move away to get me out of the picture, but asked you to spy on me. Which you did, asking colleagues to participate. All the while continuing to lie to me. How am I doing so far?"

"Your father asked me to do my job and check up on you. It has nothing to do with now."

"Your supervisor seemed to think differently. You've been suspended."

"I can deal with that later. The important thing is getting your memory restored."

"So like my father. Focused on the most important thing first. The most important thing to *you*. Not me. Never my desires." Furious, not just at herself for trusting Levi with her life, but also at him and her father. Neither had thought she could manage alone. And both thought they were right making the decision for her to enter the WITSEC program and live another lie.

She was sick of deceptions.

Forcing herself to calm down, she continued before she lost her courage. "Back in St. Louis, you said you weren't a liar. My definition must be different than yours."

"Jolene—"

"Please don't." She raised her hand to keep him on his side of the room. "Don't hug me and tell me it was for my own good. Lying by omission is still lying. What else haven't you told me?"

"There are things I can't share. I can tell you some eventually because you'll remember and then I can fill in the blanks. A lot I can never talk about because of what I do."

"I don't know whether to admire you or hate you."

"Are those the only two choices?" He took a couple of steps toward her.

Jo suddenly felt defeated or conquered. His grin had her heart and mind hoping for possibilities that could just be a ruse to get what he wanted.

"What do you want from me, Levi?"

"Nothing. Is that so hard to comprehend?" Another step her direction.

She could concentrate, her hands weren't fisted around her middle. She might actually consider herself calm. But

if she faced him…he'd see the longing in her eyes. She was sure he would. *Watch the traffic.*

"For the record, I got you into this mess and I'll get you out," her protector announced. "What did you remember at the house?"

"How is LuLu connected to the men who murdered my parents?"

"I can only guess. I'm sure you have questions, but for now, tell me what you saw and we'll work out the rest later."

"What can you do since you've been suspended?"

"I still have friends, Jo." He closed the distance between them and cupped both of her shoulders. "We'll find her. Right now, I need to know if you remembered what the *Rainbow Man* looked like."

She tried to dip her shoulder and be released from his grip, but he didn't budge. She didn't want to be this close to him. Something happened when he touched her. Her mind just went blank.

"Jo, can you picture his face?" he asked.

Levi's voice was soft or far away. She shut her eyes and the image in the kitchen flashed.

"No, his face is just a blur of colors and fog. Why can't I see?"

"You will. Don't run after it. Relax and let it come to you." He tugged her closer.

His clean smell mixed with a nice musky scent.

"The images are hard to put words to. Memories? Fantasy? It's hard to separate what's real from what I want to remember." She dropped her face to his chest, stretching her arms around his waist, just above his gun holster. His arms encircled her, protecting her. His fingertips weren't patting her in comfort. There was a difference.

It didn't matter if he hadn't shared everything or not.

This man was the only connection she had to her parents. The only person who knew the truth about her identity or who cared about helping her find the murderer.

"Tell me. Leave nothing out. I'll help. I promise, Jo, I can help."

Levi the marshal would keep her safe from murderers, but who would keep her heart safe from Levi the man?

# Chapter Nine

Jolene's fingers gently kneaded the stiff muscles in his back. A gesture she probably wasn't aware she made, but one that made it tough for Levi to not want more. Her arms tightened around his waist. In contrast, her body melted into his.

Jo was in danger.

And not only from the men chasing her.

Levi let her slip away from his arms and turn halfway back to the window. He unclipped his holster, setting the worn leather around his firearm on the nightstand. He could give her a couple of minutes. Then they had to get out of this hotel. He was stupid to bring her back here, but where else could they be dropped off by the PD?

He faced the wall, watching her worried, confused, beautiful, expressive face in the mirror to his left.

Whatever drew them together was getting stronger. He felt her next to him no matter how big the room was. Train compartment, police station or front porch. Colorado, Georgia or Texas. It didn't matter.

He had to stop thinking about her as the Jo that attracted him and think of her as Emaline Frasier, the witness who wasn't a witness. The indirect sunlight danced across her silky skin. She was still by the window and still Joseph's daughter.

His arms felt empty. He didn't know what to do with his hands so he gathered the few clothes they had and shoved them into his duffel. He itched to reach out and jerk her back to him.

God, kissing her would be the most natural thing in the world.

Then again, coaxing her to the bed would be, too. Just kissing her, having her melt into him again.

Who was he kidding? If he took her to bed, they wouldn't leave it for three days or be dead that afternoon. They couldn't stay anywhere long. Might have already been followed and compromised.

The bed was looking more and more inviting. As much as he wanted to, had always wanted to, having a relationship with a witness was against the rules.

*Sunday dinners with Joseph? Volunteering for extra duty in Atlanta so you could check on Jolene yourself? That fits your definition of a proper witness rapport?*

The harder he tried not to have a relationship, the more obvious it was that there was one. He didn't have the excuse of witness protection to deflect his feelings any longer. He was suspended and she wasn't a witness.

Yet.

He got the toothbrushes and hotel shampoo bottles. When he shoved them along with his dirty shirt into his open duffel, Jo jerked to attention, wide eyes brimming with tears. She hurriedly looked around the room, as if she hadn't seen him packing. And then she was there, tight in his arms, where she belonged.

She clung to him, sobbing. He held her, not thinking about questions, destinations or making love to her—as much as he could.

"Jo," he said across the top of her hair—much better if he didn't look into the deep green of her eyes. "I'm sorry I

couldn't tell you the truth about your dad's status. Or why you were off limits to me."

"Shh. Please don't say anything. I can't think anymore. I don't want to think. I just need to be right here. Just for a minute." Her body tightened. No longer relaxed against him, she trembled.

He'd seen the reaction before when the memories barged into her consciousness. Jolene Atkins may want to stop the memories, but Emaline Frasier was ready to let the truth be told.

"Why don't you sit?" He led her to the chair in the corner, pushing on her shoulders when she just stood as if she didn't know what to do.

Trancelike, her knees bent. She sat. She stared at her feet.

Another memory surfacing. Had to be. What had triggered this one? Holding her?

"Jo?"

"Hmm?"

"You okay?" He sat on the edge of the bed. Only two feet and yet miles away from her. He wanted to believe he could handle recovering these traumatic memories, but he was walking blind. Running. Damn, they needed to get moving. He pushed away from the soft temptation of the unmade bed.

She shook her head from side to side. Acknowledging that she'd heard him, but far away.

"We've been here too long, Jo. We've got to go."

"Where this time?"

"Not sure. We'll figure it out."

"We don't have a car anymore. We left it at the house."

He swung into his jacket, then ducked his head into the loop of his duffel back strap now tied where it had been

cut. Reminding him that his head had a lump and stitches from being taken by surprise on the train.

Not again.

Gun holstered and ready to pull when they went through the door. He was the only protection she had and he wouldn't let her down.

Levi laced his fingers with Jo's, tugged her to her feet and somehow she continued straight into his arms. Their eyes connected and he was a goner.

Each time their lips touched, the need inside him grabbed hold and wouldn't let go. It was anchored to something he didn't understand because nothing had ever reached that part of him before.

It scared him enough to run, yet spurred him forward at the same time. He tried to retreat and Jo deepened their kiss. Her mouth was a warm haven, a taste that belonged to him.

They'd been close to leaving and now they were closer to falling on that bed. But he wasn't a fool. He had a duffel on his back, a loaded gun on his hip and they were still wearing all their clothes. Just because a gorgeous brunette was pressed snug against the rest of him didn't mean he'd lose control.

He could handle this. If he could just stop kissing her.

Easier thought than accomplished.

Jo pushed at his shirt, tugged the buttons apart, holding the duffel strap high enough for him to duck his head under.

*Don't.*

He did and pressed their bodies closer. The pink pullover shirt she wore had decorative buttons. He tugged it loose from her jeans.

*Skin. Smooth, luscious skin.*

His jacket fell to the floor. It wouldn't take much maneuvering to shrug off their shirts and fall on the bed.

His fingers circled her tiny waist, moving for maximum coverage across her back. Imagining how she'd actually feel didn't compare to having her this close to him. Her shirt had to stay on or he would be completely helpless. He wrapped his hands around her shoulders. He missed the warmth and taste of her lips as soon as he turned away.

Jo may have clung to him asking not to think, but things had changed. Levi couldn't think. Not rationally. The threat got pushed to the back of his mind when his arm was timidly guided to a soft breast.

"How am I supposed to resist you?"

"You want to?" she asked with her lips against his bare skin.

He answered with another kiss. Like a hungry, starving man, he explored the feast in his arms.

*What am I doing?*

No longer ignoring the beautiful woman or the attraction they'd had since meeting. That's what.

Touching her soft curves for the first time it was inconceivable that he'd waited this long. He'd known her over four years and wanted her ever since the introduction. Witness or no witness, right now she was his.

His.

The intensity of their kisses grew. He wanted Jo's silky skin to be next to him. Feeling her warmth, seeing tan lines, freckles, the soft dip to her hip bone.

Not possible. Couldn't happen. Would eventually happen. Just not now.

Now wasn't good. They'd be rushed and he wanted a long time to explore what had been keeping him awake at nights.

Jo reacted to the intensity of the man in her arms.

She knew what was happening, but couldn't stop. Better words…she didn't *want* to stop. Levi's lips lifted from her mouth and laid smaller, intimate kisses down her neck.

He was right. They had to stop and leave the hotel. She didn't want to, but…

"I have an idea." Jolene heard her hoarse voice squeak the words out when she could get her lips to stop pursuing Levi's.

"I have one, too," he answered with an inviting smile. "Fact is if we land in that bed, I won't be protecting you very well."

The idea of sleeping with Levi sent pleasant, excited tingles everywhere. He was right, of course. They needed to leave. Leaving the protection of his arms was definitely harder to physically accomplish than think about.

The warmth of his lips on her neck shot another lustful image through her mind. Her fingers laced through his short hair, brushing the bandage where he'd been hit. He sucked a short hiss between his teeth, but pushed her shirt farther to the side, scraping her collarbone with his teeth.

*Now or never.*

"Motor home."

"Hmm?" he hummed, not lifting his mouth from her skin.

"If we could get a motor home instead of another hotel, would we be safe?"

He tossed his head back, leaving his own neck exposed for kissing, but she only skimmed a finger across his pulse point. He wrapped her hand in his, drawing it to his lips, then between them over his heart.

Her elbow rested next to his gun. A constant reminder of the danger.

"That's not a half-bad idea."

"I have them occasionally." *And you haven't asked for*

*my opinion on anything.* "It shouldn't be hard to find one around here."

"Deals like that require a lot of cash though." He kissed her fingers lightly and let go. "They don't hold a check."

She immediately longed for the warmth and security of him in spite of his smartass remark while he redressed. Following to the door, she waited when he left her a moment to search the hallway.

Darn it, she knew what she was doing. He was treating her like someone who just joined the program yesterday. Had he forgotten she'd been raised to expect this moment? He tapped again to signal it was okay to leave.

Silently, he led the way to the stairwell, holding the door, letting it click but not shut under its own force. She waited for him to take the lead. He brushed a finger across her lips before she could speak.

Silence.

No footsteps. Just the thundering of her pulse escalating in her ears.

The conversation would wait. He wasn't leaving her behind. He stepped lightly, she mimicked, longing for it all to be over.

Did he?

The late afternoon sun hit her face and she kept her silence.

They were able to leave the hotel without seeing a soul—including the police officer still in his vehicle out front. Dallas, it seemed, wasn't a city where taxis sought out fares by driving the streets. They had to be summoned. Even if there had been one, they couldn't have waltzed out the front door to stand in line.

Two blocks of parking lots on the backside of the hotel. Levi constantly turned, watched, scanned.

"Are you ready to listen to my idea?"

They were at the rear corner of a convenience store. Levi took her elbow, guiding her so her back was against the wall. He placed his arms to either side of her shoulders. Tempted as she was to put her arms around his neck and pull his mouth to hers again, she resisted.

"What were you saying about a motor home?" He kept his voice low and close to her ear.

One little half turn of her head and she'd be kissing him, headed down a path of uncontrollable cravings. "I think we could find one, buy it without being traced and we wouldn't have to worry about hotels anymore."

He laughed.

The one when he knew something she didn't. The laugh that always told her he was about to win at a board game.

She wanted to push away from his arms. Stand alone. Straight. Competent. "I can do it. Any newspaper will have one for sale by a private owner. No paper trail until you file for a title. Right?"

"One problem. No cash."

"We have plenty if you're willing to risk a trip to the bank. A quick trip. By the time they know we've been there, we'll be gone."

His lips parted with a question seemingly on the tip of a tongue she preferred tracing the sensitive spot he'd discovered at the nape of her neck.

He took a step back and scanned their surroundings again. "Just how much cash are you talking about, Jo?"

"Mother's money has gone untouched. First as an emergency exit fund, as Dad called it. Then as an inheritance I should use after I married."

His brows drew closer and closer together, his lips flat and compressed.

"Are you angry with me?" He was, she could see the tension in the corded muscles of his neck.

"No. It's a good plan. What bank?" The crooked smile stretched from cheek to cheek not quite reaching his deep-set eyes.

"You *are* mad at me."

"Not at you, Jo. Myself. I've been stupid." He shook his head, grabbed her elbow again and led her around the corner inside the gas station. "Any chance you can call us a cab?" he asked the clerk.

And that was the end of conversation. She waited at the back of the store, toward the storage room with a concrete wall behind her. Safe, according to her warden. Levi stood covertly next to a window, utilizing his stealth and height to keep watch for a potential threat. Obviously stewing.

Something had happened and she was clueless.

Maybe it was because she didn't have that much experience with people or maybe her view was clouded because she'd thought she'd known him. Whichever the reason, she felt defeated, hurt and banished to the corner.

The taxi pulled up within twenty minutes, just as the sun was setting behind them.

If she were honest with herself, sitting on those worn seats hadn't come a moment too soon. Any additional time to think and she would have been in tears from everything she'd been through that day.

A visit to her childhood home. Shot at and harbored by a stranger who was a friend of her father's. Treated almost like a criminal by the police. All the memories flooding through her yet just out of her grasp. And Levi.

Levi kissed her like no one else existed and she'd kissed him back wanting a lot more.

Jo had to think hard that it really had been just that morning she'd awoken from a drugged slumber. Just two full days ago, she'd been burying her father. Her father the landscaper.

Had she really known either man? Joseph Atkins or Robert Frasier? A simple enough answer for her. Yes. Her father was real no matter what his name. He'd loved plants, loved creating things with his hands, thoroughly disliked the day job he'd received from the Marshals Service. And more than anything else, hated the fact she hadn't had a normal childhood and a mother to answer the questions that embarrassed him on more than one occasion.

There were no doubts she loved her father or that he'd loved her.

Oh, no, she *was* going to cry.

She held it together. Hiding the silent sniffles by wrapping her arms around herself and watching the taxi join the flow of evening traffic on the highway. She hadn't heard Levi tell him where to go. It was too late to find a bank. He probably hated her idea anyway.

They turned and a beautiful clear Texas sunset full of oranges, golds and pinks filled the sky. It was beautiful. Had her father missed his Texas homeland?

She watched the colors swirl and mix, feeling sorry for herself until the image of a cartoon-like man wouldn't leave her mind. Razor-sharp angles brought his face together almost like a Japanese cartoon. His multicolored straw-like hair and the red devil eyes were from a storybook. Something she'd seen as a child.

As much as she wanted to believe that the *Rainbow Man* was real, it was becoming highly unlikely. Levi wouldn't believe her if she described him. It was the imagination of a five-year-old. No amount of sunshine shooting through crystals could create the hellish image she remembered of her mother's murderer.

# Chapter Ten

TEXT MESSAGE: Blocked Sender 7:19 P.M.
This distracting annoyance will end tomorrow. Priority is to
find and eliminate the target. No excuses will be accepted.

JO STOOD BY another third-floor window in another hotel
somewhere in another part of Dallas. More like a suburb
with a different name. It didn't matter if she was completely turned around and had no idea which direction
was which. Levi barely spoke while they paid for a rental
and drove around looking at other cheap cars to purchase
tomorrow.

Whoever followed them would know about the rental
soon. Another reason it was parked several blocks away.
Levi's plan? Buy a used car just like she'd suggested buy-
ing a motor home. A quick trip to a branch of her bank in
the morning, purchase the car, return the rental…Then?

He'd made phone calls from their "burner cell." If he'd
had explanations he hadn't shared them with her.

"Now what do we do?" she asked, desperately hoping
he had more plans. "Don't expect for me to shut everything off and go to sleep."

At least there were two beds. She didn't have to ask him
to sleep on the chair so she'd keep her hands to herself.

Then again, he hadn't exactly been the one to call their earlier kissing session to a halt.

The reassurance of his fingers curving around her shoulder didn't take her by surprise. She wanted them there next to her. She longed to trust him with decisions and with her emotions. That couldn't happen and she constantly had to remind herself that wasn't what he wanted. He'd made that very plain.

"Maybe we should talk about *this* before you turn in?" He held her mother's carving in the palm of his other hand. "You said there's a compartment?"

"Yes. Do you think she hid something inside?"

"If she did, would LuLu have known how to open it?" He handed it to her.

No more than six inches tall and three or four in diameter. She used to know what to press, hold, turn. Levi must have seen her worried expression. He covered her hands with his own, got her attention.

"Just hold it. Don't think about it."

"If that woman knew anything about this carving it was because she spied on us. My dad told me how to make it open. It was a family secret."

He removed his hands and walked around the room. "Any idea where the carving came from?"

He was a pleasure to watch. He moved like a strong, confident man. Someone used to a confined space, but who didn't enjoy them. He shrugged out of his jacket and unclipped his gun. Something she'd seen him do many times over the past couple of days. A normal action for him that didn't change his facial expression.

The concern on his face was totally for her.

She rubbed the wood with the tips of her fingers. Still warm from Levi's pocket and touch, smooth from age and other strokes of love. Sadie Colter/LuLu had said it was

filthy. She used the edge of her shirt to wipe off layers of dust and a little grime. Nothing could make it "filthy" in her mind.

"It's beautiful. Sorry, you asked if I knew where it was from. No. My mother loved and valued it. That's all I remember."

"And you think it was made specifically for your mother?"

"Absolutely. I was only allowed to look at it when she was there to help." No latches or seams separating pieces. Smooth. She continued to stroke it as she sat, keeping the artwork her mother had loved in her lap.

"I get the idea that you didn't always ask for help." He chuckled under his breath.

"My mom would put it on the highest shelf so I couldn't reach it. I'd bring toys from outside to stand on..."

The image of a tricycle and falling shot across her mind's eye. Potent. Full of the pain from hitting the handlebars on the way to the floor. She caught herself rubbing her chin, expecting the skin to be torn and open.

"That had disaster written all over it. I suppose you fell?"

"Huh?"

"Jolene, what just happened?" Levi knelt at her feet. His eyebrows drew together in concern again.

She wanted to move her stroke to his brow and brush his worry away. She'd wanted it so many times in the past, she'd been afraid to touch him. She wasn't now. His skin was warm. His expression changed from concern to curiosity, but he stayed where he was—one hand on her knee, the other caressing her hold on the wooden puppy.

She liked his smile the best, even if he was troubled about her reactions to her memories. He was so determined that she remember and go into the WITSEC pro-

gram. She needed to tell him again that wasn't an option. She wouldn't spend the rest of her life looking over her shoulder or wondering if she made a mistake that would cost the lives of the ones she loved.

"You okay?" he asked, his grip firmer, offering encouragement.

"You're right. I fell and cut my chin trying to get to this hunk of wood."

He tipped her head toward the ceiling, his thumb rubbed where her own fingers had been moments before. She closed her eyes and felt his knuckle drag the length of her throat. "No scar."

Levi's hands went to the arms of the chair and he half stood, leaning toward her. His face inched closer. His lips were warm, firm, in charge and she welcomed the need she recognized. She wanted so much more. Wanted...

She heard a click. Or felt it in her hands.

Levi moved back, looking at her lap. The carved dog statue was in two pieces, having come apart at the dog's collar. Relaxed, without thinking, her fingers had worked the mechanism.

"Nice." He sat on the bed, removed his shoes and tossed them to the other side of the room.

"It's empty."

"That was to be expected. They wouldn't have handed it back to us any other way." He slapped his thighs. "Ready to tell me what you remembered today?"

"It was just today?"

"Yeah, a lot's happened."

"I guess it has." She'd rather talk about the touching and kisses. She'd postponed telling him her jumbled memories long enough, but didn't believe she could get through all of the emotional stress without breaking down. "Honestly,

I'm exhausted. Which bed's mine and how early do I have to get up? Can we do it in the morning when—"

"One more thing." Levi crossed the room and sifted through his duffel, setting items on the dresser until he removed the manila envelope where her father's letters were stored. "Part of my instructions was to give you this whenever I felt the timing was right."

He turned to her and in his hand was a second wooden statue of a dog. At first glance it looked identical to the one in pieces still in her hands. They were a set of cocker spaniels, both carved by the same person.

"I had to be careful not to interfere with what you were remembering. We haven't exactly had a lot of time for discussion."

"Give it to me." Her eyes filled with tears. Her mind filled with confusion. She took a step to meet him, grabbed the dog and ran to the bathroom with both.

Levi could open the door easily, busting through or opening the lock, but he wouldn't. Jo closed the toilet lid, threw a towel around her chilled shoulders and sat. She stared into the plaster on the wall. Counted the number of tiles on the floor and cracks in the ceiling. All the while, running her fingers over and around the small statue.

"Jo? You've been in there over thirty minutes."

If the circumstances weren't so extreme, she'd wonder about the amount of time she'd spent in baths lately. "Go to bed. I'm not going anywhere."

"I know that."

"Leave me alone. Please."

There was a long string of curses on the other side of the thin door. "That doesn't appear to be in my nature where you're concerned."

Her heart could read a lot into that statement, but her head kept reminding her that Levi Cooper held a lot of in-

formation about her parents. More secrets. And the more she learned, the harder it was to forgive.

Two hours and Jo hadn't budged from the bathroom. And Levi hadn't budged from his spot in front of the door. Two nice-sized beds wasted and his backside was numb. Had been numb for over an hour.

If he stretched out on the inviting bed, he might not hear her sneak out. He hadn't slept much since the night before the funeral and couldn't take the chance.

"Come on, Jo." He tried one last time, then he was putting the pillow he sat on under his head, blocking the doors and grabbing some much-needed shuteye. "There wasn't much I could do except follow your dad's instructions. It might have kept you from remembering anything."

She was probably asleep, curled up in a small ball on the floor, covered with a towel or cramped in the tub. He'd spent a couple of nights in a tub. Not fun.

A click. A creak.

An exhausted-looking, red-eyed Jolene peeked around the edge of the partially opened door. He kept his mouth shut. She looked like she'd been crying the entire time she'd been in there.

"I can't figure out how to open it. I thought if I held it like the other one that something would happen. I mean, I didn't think about opening the other statue, so why would this one be any different?"

Harder to keep his mouth shut and wait. She came to him, wooden dog outstretched in her hand, gesturing for him to take it from her.

"I thought it was a message from my dad. Or a clue. Something important that would help. Or just something that he wanted me to have."

He took the dog, dropped it on the pillow, then pulled her into his arms.

"He wanted you to have it, Jo. We'll figure out why later. You're too tired."

"I couldn't do it." Her body shook with her tears and grief.

Levi should have been prepared for it. Over the past couple of days he'd gone through the different things that could have been happening behind the closed door. "You're exhausted and need some rest."

She looked up from his chest with her swollen eyes. "I have to help my dad."

He brought her cheek back to his T-shirt. "Honey, the last thing your father wanted was for you to blame yourself. Rest. We can find the answers tomorrow."

"I wish I could believe you."

"I wish you could, too."

If she wouldn't get in bed he'd take her there himself. Lifting her into his arms was no trouble, even as tired as he was. She didn't protest. Her arms circled tightly around his neck, and if they hadn't, he would have thought she was asleep in a couple of steps. He kept her in his arms and tugged the sheet enough to get her covered.

The door was locked.

They were safe…for a while.

Like he'd told Jo, nothing to do except get some rest. After some much-needed sleep, they could determine their next move with clearer heads.

His witness who wasn't a witness turned on her side and pulled her hands under her chin. Sleep. He wanted it, needed it, couldn't function without it. He grabbed the spread off the empty double bed behind him and carefully lay down next to Jo.

He wouldn't sleep worried about her leaving without

him. Better to worry about keeping his hands off her instead.

The bed was a little crowded, his feet hung off the bottom a bit. He stared at the light intruding from the curtains' edge and bouncing around on the ceiling. He'd just closed his eyes when Jo rolled over and snuggled next to his side. She released a long relaxed sigh.

Levi pulled her in close, reluctant to ever let her go. Knowing that it was the only way she'd ever be safe.

LEVI'S MOMENT OF rest and safety was gone. Replaced by a crazy minute of thinking that he was screwed. As he listened to the jumble of memories Jolene had experienced in the last couple of days, he did have a split second of wavering and asking himself: *Was it worth it?*

Was the *woman* he'd woken up with worth it?

*Yes.*

There was no doubt he'd make the same decision to protect and help her.

As she'd filled him in on the crazy thoughts and when they'd happened, she nervously twisted the end of her shirt, clicked her nails on her chin a few times until she noticed what she was doing, and then wrapped her arms around her midsection. It was her thing. Her nervous "tell."

Easy to read and easy to care about. Innocent people always were, but it was more. He liked Jolene Atkins and had to get past that.

What was best for the witness?

"We need a plan. A couple of them. Restoring your memory has to be a priority." He watched her cover her face and shake her head.

"I've been attempting to prioritize. Really. It's a jumbled mess and easier to think about the person who wants to

kill me than solving my mother's murder. Which is such a long shot."

"We'll find the person responsible."

"Levi, I just told you that my mother's murderer looks like a Japanese anime cartoon. There's not much hope of finding him." Frustrated, her hands went in the air, then one fist lightly pounded the edge of the dresser.

"I heard you."

"Well?" she asked without facing him.

"Well...I think we should grab that continental breakfast before heading to the car."

"That's not quite the discussion I anticipated."

"There's not much more we can do here. We can form a plan of action in the car. Speaking of which, they may have already found—"

She whirled around, indicating with her hands for him to stop. It worked.

"Levi, you have to face the fact that I may not remember. I may always think the man holding a gun to my mother's head had green-and-blue straw hair and a pointed nose from something in a Tim Burton film." She plopped onto the bed and covered her face. "I can't do this."

"What? Stay alive? 'Cause I don't remember giving you a choice. Did you think it would be easy?"

He didn't believe Jo was a quitter. They'd been forced into an impossible situation. He knew she could handle anything. She just didn't have experience with avoiding killers.

"What I thought is that I'd bury my father who died in a car accident last week and return to my boring job in Georgia yesterday. *That's* what I thought. I don't want to run and hide for the rest of my life."

She wasn't crying. She seemed almost angry at him.

Okay, he had led the shooter to her in St. Louis. Crap, he'd lost her on the train, too.

"No one said it would be easy." He offered a hand, wanting to pull her close and make everything okay.

She slapped it away, standing on her own. "Don't *handle* me. I'm not one of your…your witnesses."

Maybe holding her would make *him* feel better. It wasn't the professional solution. Just desire and the reaction to holding her all night. "I thought I was treating you like a person who needed my expertise and help."

"Right." She marched to the door, obviously hurt and upset.

"What did I say?"

Jo did an about-face, poking him in the chest with a fingernail. He took a step back and she let the door close hard enough that he was glad they were about to leave 'cause someone would be calling the manager.

"Pay attention, *Marshal Dillon, sir.*"

"I really don't like that name."

"Sorry, but you need to do more than just listen. Believe me. No matter how this turns out, I am not returning to the WITSEC program. Ever. My dad taught me how to be safe, but he also taught me how not to live. I'm done with that."

"There's no other—"

"Shush. I'm not finished." She poked his chest again. She paced several steps, her hands on her slender hips, then pushed one through her short hair, ruffling it into rippling waves. "I have lived more almost dying for the past three days than I have my entire existence. I don't want to live the rest of my life on the run, but that doesn't mean I won't."

She stood in front of him, appearing confident and sure of herself. He heard the words, felt her conviction, understood she was afraid in spite of her bravado.

"You may think you know me, Levi Cooper, but you don't. Count on this…I am not returning with you to Denver. I am not running to witness protection, even if I remember more than *Rainbow Man*. I will not spend the rest of my life lying and not living."

He'd been shushed and kept his thoughts to himself. Because he knew what was involved in her dream. Knew that she had no clue what she was up against.

"I'm not a child or just Joseph's daughter. You've been holding pieces of this puzzle from me and I don't want any more surprises. At least not from you."

It was past time he told her the whole truth.

Damn the consequences.

"Are you done?" he asked, noticing that his teeth hurt from clenching his jaw.

She nodded, wide green eyes reflecting the anger that perched on the tip of his tongue. He didn't blame her.

"Sit down."

"I don't want—"

"I don't care. So sit."

She pressed her lips together and sat. Not in the chair, on the bed. "You sit, too."

He dropped the duffel to the floor and deliberately walked to the window. As far as he could see, no one watched the room. "I don't like being on our own here. Protecting you is a full-time, round-the-clock job."

"No one asked you to."

"Yes, he did, Jolene." Sadly, he recalled the day Joseph had pleaded for his word. The last time he'd seen him alive. That story was for another day.

"I mean…I know you said Dad…Sorry."

"Here's what you don't know." He shoved the hair falling on his forehead back with the rest. Dammit, he hated this. "Six months ago I received a flag on your father's

case. The weapon used to shoot him and kill two marshals was used in a random killing in Dallas."

"What does 'random' mean?"

"Good question. As far as I could tell, this shooting had nothing to do with your family's case, and quite frankly there didn't seem to be a reason why the convenience store clerk had been killed. Which in itself set off red flags for me. As much as I wanted to get involved—to investigate myself—there was no indication of a connection. Don't give me that look like it was unimportant because it involved your family. That old gun was used to shoot and kill two of our own. The Marshals Service took the investigation very seriously and found nothing. Just a matching ballistics report."

"You already mentioned that the gun had been used. If there's no connection, how does that matter to us now?"

"I've had time to think. I have no proof, but I believe the gun was a lure to get your father to Dallas."

"But everyone thought he was dead."

"Someone outside the Marshals Service knew your father was alive and still a threat that needed to be eliminated."

She came to him at the window. The filtered morning light darkened her hair and made her skin glow. The worry settled on her forehead and in her direct steps to his arms.

The pull between them—lust or grief—was real and constant.

"But you said it yourself, Levi, he's been safe for twenty years. Who would want to kill him now?"

"The murderer."

# Chapter Eleven

TEXT MESSAGE: Blocked Sender 07:18 A.M.
KILL THEM NOW!

IN LEVI'S ARMS, Jo felt much safer than his constant reminders to the contrary should have encouraged. Their discussion would progress faster if they separated and each paced different areas of the hotel room.

The small space seemed to be shrinking when she moved to the opposite wall. Levi's presence dwarfed everything else around him. Or it might have been her desire to be in his arms, protected.

No, she could fight this feeling. Stay clear of physical contact and fight her urges. Agree with him sending her away once they found her mother's evidence. Let him believe she'd return to witness protection. After this was said and done, she could take care of herself.

*That can be my secret.*

She fluffed her short hair, still drying from her quick shower. Levi hadn't seen it this length. She'd cut it since her last visit home. He hadn't mentioned it. He actually hadn't mentioned much at all. Not where he or his family or his real life was concerned.

Something else to ask about later, when life wasn't chas-

ing them in circles. Stop thinking about Levi. Concentrate on the facts.

"You think my mother's murderer committed another murder six months ago to draw my father into the open. Honestly, my father was left for dead. For all purposes he did die. This case has gone without scrutiny for so long. It doesn't make sense to take that risk. Using the weapon that killed those marshals seems illogical. The killers wouldn't know if my father had access to the ballistics reports."

"It was in the papers, made national news. Maybe it was a test to see if someone was still watching? Or a threat to a person like LuLu, for instance. Perhaps reestablishing who was in control."

"It would be smarter to destroy the gun and let sleeping dogs lie."

"Unless the dog was already rousing." He paced the length of the room. "From the beginning. Elaine Frasier, big shot attorney comes across something so scary she's willing to give up her career, the life she knows and protect her family by entering WITSEC."

"You're positive the Department of Justice didn't have a name and as a result of investigating all her clients no dirty laundry was aired?"

"That's right. So what could she have found? And where's the evidence?"

"Why do we assume there's evidence?"

"Someone thinks it exists. They wanted your dad dead."

"Why assume we can find it after twenty years?"

"Instinct? I don't know. I could be way off." He shrugged. "They've searched your family's home. If it were in Dallas, they would have found it."

"Or they simply wanted the witness to the murder dead to eliminate the possibility of exposure."

"Good point. Nothing was in the house. If your dad

had found anything he would have turned it over to protect you." He shook his head. "No arguments. I knew your dad."

*I thought I had.*

"Did the FBI consider the murderer was out for revenge?"

"There's nothing in the file to suggest that. We assume that he wants all of your family dead."

"Who could hate anyone that much?" she asked, not understanding.

"Plenty of people. Thing is, we're out of leads. I can make a call for information. I just want to make certain we've exhausted our options."

"There's still the dog statue. We can break it open." The terror that he'd actually agree was plain in her voice and on her face—she could see it in the mirror.

"Let's try an X-ray. Don't worry, I can twist an arm or ask for a favor to get it done."

"Thank you."

For their conversation he'd leaned against the open wall, arms crossed, balanced with his ankles crossed. Relaxed. And each time she looked at his body or watched the genuine concern in his eyes…She wanted to be closer.

"Wait a minute. That means no one really knows why my mother was murdered. Why didn't I realize that before?"

She'd assumed a lot of things over the years—a lot to do with her father's avoidance. But she'd never asked, avoiding quite a bit on her own. It was easier, less complicated.

Now she needed answers. She'd closed her eyes and Levi had crossed the room. These moments of unawareness—almost blackouts—were beginning to unnerve her.

"I have to see this through, Levi."

He nodded. "I don't agree with Joseph's actions and I

hate the results, but I can understand why he wanted to know. Why you want to know."

Comforting hands sought her shoulders again. Soon she'd be seeking the comfort of his lips instead of more of the story. Levi must have thought the same thing. The indecision played on his own expression before he moved back to the window doing his constant watch for danger.

The window shattered.

His body dropped like lightning to the floor.

*Oh, my God, he's been shot!*

"Get back. Inside wall. Bathroom if you can." His gun was in his hand. Prepared. Waiting.

"Are you hurt?"

"Go. Now."

He'd told her several times he couldn't protect them worrying about her. She obeyed, crawling on the floor, dragging his duffel behind her. No matter what happened, they couldn't lose the few things they had. Especially the dogs. As soon as she was on the other side of the wall that formed the open closet area she heard a string of curses. Curses aimed at the shooter, at Levi's lax protocol. They'd been located because they'd been talking instead of moving. Putting her in danger instead of keeping her safe.

"I can't see where the shooter's at."

On her belly, she looked around the divider wall. Levi was at the edge of the window. No blood on his shirt, so he hadn't been shot. More of the window burst.

What could she do? She searched the pockets of the duffel, found her battery and slipped it in her phone. Precious seconds ticked by while the cell booted up before she could dial 911.

"There's a lot of smoke on the fifth floor at the Spanish Comfort Inn on 635 and Gross Road. Please send help."

"Quick thinking. Call the front desk, tell them the same

thing." He swiped at a scratch caused from the broken glass.

She stood in the corner, well out of range of the windows and found the hotel number, dialed and told them the same story. The memory of the train was so vibrant in her mind, she nearly smelled the smoke. Before she crouched on the floor she heard the hotel fire alarm sound.

"If the police detain us again, my superiors won't be as forgiving," Levi said from the window.

"Then let's get out of here." She shut off her phone and removed the battery, replacing both in the bag. "A police escort is not an option."

When he'd hit the floor, something in her had crashed, too. She couldn't lose him. Not yet. Involving the police would separate them and stop their investigation.

"Jo, they could be waiting outside the door. We don't know if the shooter's working alone."

He moved the curtains. Another shot hit the far wall.

Levi army crawled across the carpet to her, gun still in his right hand. "You stay behind me and do exactly what I tell you to do. We wait. We look. We're careful. We stay alive."

"Right."

He smiled crookedly, comforting every part of her nervousness. "Hand me the dang duffel." He ducked into the hallway, tapping when it was okay to follow.

Sirens. If the shooter was still out front, he wouldn't be for long. Levi gave a signal for her to wait behind a cleaning cart. He checked the stairwell, stuck a hand through the door and waved for her to follow.

She felt the adrenaline rushing through her system. The uncertainty of what was around the next corner or if they'd avoid those searching for them had her heart battering her ribs as she followed Levi down two flights of stairs.

Other guests ran into them, more just walked and complained about hotel fire drills. Others didn't seem concerned, walking at a normal pace, laughing and joking like everything was normal.

Normal? Had she really thought that she wanted a normal life? She'd had that in spades in Georgia. An occasional boring date with a boring man. A job sitting in front of a boring computer all day. A social life where her limited friends met for a movie or to hear a band once a week.

What did Levi do on his night off?

"I assume it's not safe to go back to the car and we're on foot," she whispered, leaning in closer, careful not to touch her protector's back and distract him further.

He didn't speak, just gave her a look like she was crazy for asking.

On the first floor of the building, a maid had left a room door propped open facing the front of the hotel. They darted inside, and Levi gestured her to the bath area while he took a look out the window.

"Firefighters are entering the building. We've got to get to the back exit and avoid everyone."

"Okay."

With his gun just inside his jacket, Levi led her silently past the elevator and detoured into the kitchen. They received one or two suspicious looks from staff who weren't listening to the fire alarms. But no one stopped them or pretended to care. Once outside, they stayed close against the building, rounding corners that returned them to the main parking lot.

Her mind moved to the next problem of transportation until an arm circled her neck, yanking her backward to an abrupt halt.

"Drop your weapon," a muffled voice said past her ear.

Levi raised his hands. His gun still in its holster.

"I meant what I said. Two finger it to the ground."

"Not happening." Levi turned to face her attacker.

*What? Didn't they always give up their weapon in the movies?*

"Let her go."

"That's not happening either, friend."

She was hauled back against a body that seemed to be as tall as Levi and just as strong. The gun barrel hot against her skin kept her in check. She didn't know what to do. Her mind was spinning so fast she couldn't grasp anything.

"I'm taking the girl. Stay put."

The paralyzing moment of fear fled when she lost her footing in the loose gravel. The man jerked her backward to leave with him, cutting off oxygen with his thick forearm. Her feet scrambled to push against something to relieve the pressure against her windpipe. Her hands dug into his jacketed arm.

Somehow she saw Levi dip his chin, his eyes darting to his hand. Three fingers. *What?* Two fingers. She pushed harder to remove the pressure around her neck. One finger pointing to the ground. *Fall? Choke?*

She stopped trying to maintain her balance and went limp. She couldn't breathe. The man stumbled, let her go. Levi fired and leapt over her. She didn't see what happened. Her eyes closed. She coughed. She heard another shot, then Levi was back, lifting her. She latched her arms around his neck and saw a crowd of hotel guests gathering out front as he ran.

He turned behind the next building and they were out of sight.

"You can put me down now."

"Are you sure?" He released her, facing him, his arms around her, holding her close. "We can rest a minute. Let you catch your breath."

"I'm fine. You're the one who's been running." She laced her fingers with his and gave an ineffective push to get started. "Let's get out of here."

He raised his free hand and skimmed her neck. "Does it hurt?"

"No, I'm really okay." His caring touch activated something, making her forget the danger and reminding her how much she wanted to kiss him. They were still in trouble. "Did you have to...you know, kill him?"

"I might have winged him, but he was running away fast enough to assure he wasn't dead."

They walked, hand in hand around the building and watched a police car speed by.

"Thanks for saving my life again."

"No thanks needed. I'm also the guy who put you in harm's way...again."

Levi kept his hand on his holstered weapon, kept his head surveilling every direction. She'd known they hadn't been in the best part of Dallas but not many people seemed concerned that fire engines and police cars gathered just down the street.

Jo matched him stride for stride walking the broken sidewalk, beginning to feel winded from the pace or the nerves from being attacked. Looking ahead she saw a gas station, but better yet, a branch of her bank was across the intersection.

Her idea would work. She just had to convince the Marshal next to her and they wouldn't have to register at hotels again.

"Motor home, here we come."

IT HAD BEEN an easy decision for the motor home owner. Cash did that to people. It had been risky, but would solve their sleeping arrangements for a while. Bedroom for her.

Couch for him. Noble thoughts he had every intention of keeping. Levi had berated himself for the past several hours. Seemed all he did was take risks with Jolene.

A bank two blocks from where they'd been spotted. A withdrawal from an account the murderer probably knew about—*he* hadn't known but with their run of luck, the perps probably did. The local paper, another walk through an unsavory neighborhood, a couple of cabs and wham they'd purchased the first motor home they could drive away that wasn't the size of a bus.

One stop at a superstore in Mesquite gave them new burner phones and food. They'd even grabbed clean jeans, jackets and T-shirts.

Jo hadn't been exaggerating about the amount of cash in her inheritance fund. Joseph had been a very smart man, planning for his daughter's future or safety. He'd also taught her how to take care of herself. But it wasn't the first time in the past three days Levi had wished the man had been smarter about looking for Elaine's murderers.

The call connecting him to the FBI felt like he was exposing them to death rays with every minute that ticked by. The chances that someone could make a connection between him and an FBI agent he'd met twice were slim, but he still wanted off the phone.

"Special Agent George Lanning."

"George, Levi Cooper. I'm in the area and need an in-person favor. Can we meet? Very public and somewhere you normally go."

"Cowboys Red River. We dance there on Thursdays," George answered. "Nine o'clock, inside, midway on the right near the mechanical bull. I'll find you."

Another risk, bringing someone he barely knew to help Jo. He had no choice. They needed information and if he

went to anyone in the Marshals Service his gut told him the murderers would find them.

"Red River's less than twenty minutes from here," he told Jo after he disconnected.

"I still can't believe there's a motor home park so close to Dallas."

"Yeah, but you heard the manager, they get a lot of tourists."

"I wouldn't mind seeing the States in this contraption." She looked from the front closed curtains to the closed bedroom door. "Of course, I'd probably want to *see* a bit more of it along the way."

Her mood had brightened since they'd made the purchase. *Maybe because she'd made the suggestion and you actually listened to her?*

"It's better if you stay out of sight."

"I'm teasing you Marshall Dil—Levi. I know why I sat in the back. I know why the curtains are closed."

Her mother's file was under her palm, flat on the table, waiting to be opened. As much as Jolene had expressed that she wanted to read its contents, she hadn't glanced inside. He'd removed the photos. No child should see their mother like that. He didn't feel right about getting her to remember it on her own. But there was no choice.

"Jo…"

"I know, I have to look. We have to go through it. We have to find the *Rainbow Man*."

"There's a possibility he's out of the picture. He could be dead, skipped the country."

"You don't believe that, either," she said, sounding miserable.

"We have six hours to kill before we meet George. What would you like to do?" He slid onto the bench seat next to her. Aching to drop his arm around her shoulder. Won-

dering if it were the right thing to do. They needed to talk about the file, about a plan, about what would happen if she didn't remember.

He didn't want to talk.

"We could explore," she said, scrapping her fingernail across her bottom lip.

She had no clue what she did to his blood flow. Explore? Yeah, he wanted to explore her silky skin and discover every freckle, scar or goose flesh she might develop when he had her naked and stretched across the bed.

Six hours to explore. Heaven or hell?

Her hands rubbed her thighs. Her lips parted. "I'm dying to get outside for a while. How about you?"

*Torture.*

"Walking or running?" he asked, dreading the answer, dreading the delay.

They wanted each other and he was tired of denying it. He couldn't pretend she was off-limits much longer.

"I think I'm too drained for a run and going in circles around the drive isn't really what I had in mind anyway." She lifted the corner of the folder.

Jo wasn't making a move to open the file and didn't seem to be in a hurry to get out the door. Did she want him to make a decision for her?

Normally, he was an intuitive guy. His fellow marshals trusted his instincts. With Jo, he was a clueless idiot, sitting on his hands, waiting for the perfect moment that would never come.

"A walk around the park then?" He turned to her, met her eyes. She actually seemed a little irritated. He backed off the bench, not losing eye contact, following those beautiful orbs right to the moment her lips locked on his.

Normally intuitive? Never with this woman.

Jolene launched herself at her thickheaded protector.

The only running she desired was her fingers through Levi's thick, short hair. The man's lips devoured her. One hand at her nape kept her mouth against his. The excitement shooting through her body built and needed more.

More of him against her. More of her against him.

Levi moved his lips to her neck, pushing aside the T-shirt.

"We could get this out of your way." She lifted the hem. *Be bold. Tell him what you want.*

"No waiting, huh?" He tilted his head back and half smiled like he knew something she didn't again.

She loved and hated that grin all at once. And just as sure as she'd been a few moments before, she was completely uncertain now. Did he know just how many guys she hadn't slept with and how inexperienced she was?

She shrugged, completely unsure how to proceed with this contradictory man who knew too much about her life. "We can do whatever."

"Fast is good," he said and pulled her shirt over her head, following with his own. "Time for slow later."

His thumbs brushed her breasts through the lacy bra. The sensation spiked straight through to her spine like lightning sparking on a cloudless night. She closed her eyes and imagined herself as someone brave and bold. Someone who went after what she wanted.

Without feeling it happen, she was topless and longing to feel her skin pressed against his hot bare flesh. She shoved at Levi's shirt, pushing it over his shoulders. Her fingers returned to tour the light dusting of chest hair she'd wanted to touch for days.

His hands skimmed her sides and tugged at her jeans while her fingers were on a quest of their own discovering the contours of each muscle she'd ever admired.

No words. No talking. If they said anything he might

try to convince her it wasn't right, convincing himself again that it shouldn't happen. But everything was perfect. Every stroke, every touch, every bit of the frenzy and heart-pumping excitement she felt.

Whatever he'd meant to do before right now, Levi's body reacted to her hand on his zipper. He sucked in a long breath and pressed their bodies together.

They tugged, tripped and stepped from their shoes and jeans until they were skin to skin at the edge of the bed.

"You sure you want this?" Levi asked her.

"You're the one who's been turning me down," she said, laughing. "Really, Levi, shouldn't you be saying something along the lines of how beautiful I am?"

"You're beautiful and I'm an idiot for waiting all this time."

"Shh." She laid her finger across his lips.

"Beautiful and bossy."

There was nothing rushed in the way he gently lay her on the bed or slowed their frenzied touching to luxurious lovemaking.

She'd been wrong about a lot of things since her father had died. But there was a prediction she'd made with scary accuracy. No one could protect her heart from the man in her arms. He'd stolen it straight from the protection of her chest.

Somewhere during the four years they'd known each other, she'd fallen in love with Levi Cooper, the U.S. Marshal. But when it came to Levi the man, she knew absolutely nothing.

# Chapter Twelve

Levi flipped her underneath him, causing the motor home to sway slightly. He'd agreed that fast was good but evidently had changed his mind since his lips lingered at her neck while his fingers intertwined with hers.

He gently scraped his bristled cheek across her shoulder to her breasts.

How could he drive her this crazy with just a five o'clock shadow delighting her skin?

"Levi, didn't you say fast was good?" She tugged her hands, trying to escape for her own survey. Tugging again, he gently held her closer, scraping her taut nipples with his cheek stubble, making her more sensitive with every pass.

"Slow has a few good points all its own," he whispered.

She wanted to touch him and he knew it. When he returned to nibbling her neck she wrapped one leg around his hip and pressed against him. Her breasts flattened under the muscles she adored as she arched to rekindle some of their intensity.

"Guess we aren't playing fair, then?" he whispered and teased her ear.

That sound lightened her heart and brought a smile to her lips. She hadn't heard him relaxed since…well, since her last visit to Boulder.

When they'd kissed on the train and in the hotel, it was

edgy and forbidden. His body had been strong, unyielding, on guard. Here on this lumpy mattress, his hot lean frame melted her into every sculpted, manly curve.

And she wanted more. Lots more.

*Beautiful and bossy.*

His words echoed. She could do bossy. "My turn."

With her hands free, she discovered and embraced one corded muscle at a time. Lingered over Levi's shoulders and biceps. Amazed at his strength and even more impressed how he was holding back.

Levi touched her everywhere with fingertips, lips, breath, even his eyes. His feathery touch skimmed up her arms and across her ribs, while his rough chin tickled the hollow at her neck and his leg created wonderful thrills on its own.

Her whole body tingled in anticipation of his next move.

And then the anticipation was gone. The thrill of being touched in all the right places culminated in one great build of tension shattering her into a thousand pieces.

"Your turn," she said when she could force her voice to work again. "Definitely, your turn."

He rolled over her in the tight space of what the owner had said was a very good-sized bed for a motor home. But again, Levi had a habit of filling her space with his presence. He reached over the edge of the bed, fumbling through their clothing.

"I…try the drawer under the bed," she said, knowing he searched for protection. "I grabbed some from the store earlier."

"Funny." He grinned, coming back with a packet in hand. "So did I."

So the U.S. Marshal who tried his best to treat her as a witness had been thinking about her as a lover, too. If she

hadn't been warmed-over butter in his hands before, she certainly was now.

Levi set her on top of him. She was more than ready to finish what they'd started. Or begin a new part of their lives. But she was unprepared for the connection she experienced when he entered her body, her mind and her heart.

PROPPED UP WITH a pillow under her elbow, Jolene drew concentric circles on his chest with her nails. Caressing, almost tickling his skin, it was hard not to jump and let her know how much her touch affected him. He looked at the delicate skin of her throat, no bruises to remind him how close she'd come again to disappearing or even dying.

He wanted to say something profound or just tuck her under his arm and hope she understood how much he cared. But nothing would change. She was in danger and it was about to get worse.

He must have opened his mouth while trying to figure out what to say. Jo laid a finger across his lips, rising up to look through his soul.

"If you're about to apologize for what just happened, I hope you rethink opening your mouth. Or at least rethink what you should do with it."

Levi sucked her nail between his lips and caused her to shiver dramatically next to him.

She'd read his mind because an apology had been a split second from happening. Apologize for taking advantage of her or the situation or say something stupid like their sleeping together had been a lapse in his judgment.

Lies. No errors. No lapses. And nothing wrong about the way their bodies knew each other. Then or now.

"So you should just rest quietly. Unless you're ready to start over?" Her hand skimmed his chest and lower. They

still had five hours before they needed to leave. Five more hours of "exploring."

"Levi?"

"Hmm?" He took her hand in his and began kissing his way up her arm. A classic move, but he'd promised himself a look at every freckle. "Were you going to ask me something?"

"Oh, yeah." She visibly shivered again, the kind that lets a guy know he's doing something right. "I don't know… Oh, my goodness."

Levi nibbled longer on the inside of her elbow, nipping and receiving more shivers through her gorgeous body. "You were saying?"

"You know everything about me. More than you should because of your extra eyes on me in Georgia."

He let his lips wander to her taut stomach. Yeah, he knew she worked out three or four times a week to keep it as tight as it was. He liked the hard, yet feminine muscles she'd developed.

"There are a few things I don't know about." His hand wandered lower and her body arched to meet him.

"Wait." She sat up and pulled a pillow to hide behind.

"What's wrong?"

She hugged that pillow like she'd erected an electrical fence. "I'm serious."

"I'm confused." He thought she'd been directing their lovemaking and thought he'd done what she wanted. Maybe he was wrong?

"My world has no secrets and I don't even know the first thing about yours."

"Is that all? I thought I'd done something you didn't like."

"This is important, Levi."

"You're right and wrong."

"Now I don't understand."

"I have no idea how you'll react to, say, this." He threw her protective layer of pillow to the floor and pulled her on top of him. She straddled his legs, her delicate hands splaying his chest. "You're still in charge. Interrogate as much as you can before I escape."

"Bru-ha-ha. I have you in my evil clutches," she wiggled her bottom, "and you must answer all my questions truthfully."

"Cross my heart." He drew an *X* between her breasts, dragging his knuckles across her puckered nipple before returning his hand to her hips. "What do you want to know?"

If he could only tell her how much he wanted her heart to be his. He would when this mess was over. When they had the answers and no one was trying to kill her. Things would be different.

"Do you like ice cream?"

She could ask him anything and that's what she wanted to know? He could play along. "Yes."

"And what about artichokes?"

He nodded. "From what I've had in Italian food, sure."

"So you like Italian then?" She bounced excitedly on his legs.

"What man doesn't like…pasta?" Or the feast before him.

"Your middle name is…"

"Gene."

"Okay. Really?" she asked after a major pause.

"Yeah, got that a lot as a kid. I was named after my two grandfathers. My dad never thought about it 'til someone else read my name out loud."

"Cute. Where were you born? What about family? Do they know what you do?"

Her hands were making it hard to concentrate on words. But he understood her need for a connection to him. He'd held back a lot over the past four years. "Jo, I haven't lied about my attraction to you."

"Just…" She kissed his mouth. "Answer…" Then his chin, her breasts barely touched his body. "Please…" Then a kiss to his chest. "There are rewards for quick responses."

He could tell. "Amarillo. Yes. Not really." He tried to tug her back for another kiss, but she blocked his movements and crossed her arms—a reward in itself. "All right. My aunt knows I work for the Marshals Service and assumes I work with the Witness Protection division because I can't talk about my work. No more talk of family in bed."

He wanted to take advantage of Jo's position and the hours they had to spend on this thin mattress. Talk of either of their families would stop their fun faster than a nun walking into the room. His partner seemed to understand and continued her own touching exploration.

"So you're a Texan?" She sat straight again, her body sleek and inviting.

"Born and bred."

"Ever ride a horse?" she asked impishly.

"Goes without saying in my part of Texas." He hadn't ridden since high school but didn't think that mattered.

"So you were a cowboy?"

"Enough with the questions." He reached for her and she avoided his grasp.

"So you don't feel like having your life under a microscope?"

"What I feel like…is kissing you." He snagged her shoulders and quickly pulled her mouth to his, stopping the questions he didn't mind answering.

Her softened lips heated. He'd never get enough of how she tasted. He felt satisfied and yet wanted more of her. It

was a conflict he'd never experienced before. He'd never thought about…contentment.

"Later. You aren't getting off that easy," she said between a few short pants and opening herself to him again.

He laughed, unable to control the burst of simple pleasure. They had a few hours of safety. He wasn't going to waste it thinking about what they might be doing. He wanted her here, in the moment with him.

His body hovered as his guilt led him beyond Jolene's arms. What would happen next week? Or after that? The years of telling himself he couldn't have a relationship, especially Jo, overrode what his body wanted.

"Hey there, where did you go?" Jo clipped him gently on the chin.

"Maybe we should—" Stopping was the last thing he wanted. He already ached to be a part of her again.

"Shh, Levi. No what-ifs. There's just right now. This minute. This wasn't a spur-of-the-moment act. It's been four years in the making. And judging by the number of condoms we both bought…"

*Right now.*

Her words made light of this moment but her sensitive eyes said how much she needed him. And no matter what his head knew as fact, his body couldn't hide from Jo again. He'd make love with her every minute they had together.

Two boxes may not be enough.

# Chapter Thirteen

"Do you dance?" Jo asked.

She'd kept the questions coming nonstop, even from her shower. Something he would love to experience with her, but in the motor home he barely fit in the tight space by himself.

"You going to let up on the Q and A sometime tonight?"

They were at the dance hall. Huge. Lots of potential problems. Not enough exits to his liking. People hanging outside the doors, grabbing a smoke. Bystanders or the men following them? He should have thought this through a little longer before agreeing to this place.

Every head that followed them around the room was a potential threat.

"Look, it's a disco ball in the shape of a saddle." She giggled. The lights reflecting off the mirrors made her eyes shine even brighter. "You know my father never allowed me to dance." She said it wide-eyed and innocent like he should believe her. "What if we need to blend in?"

"We wouldn't want to blow our cover. Looks like I'll have to teach you a couple of steps." He wanted to dance with her, hold her close. They both knew she was a very good dancer. He'd seen her a couple of times when Joseph had asked him to escort her home.

No, Joseph hadn't encouraged it, but she'd experienced a bit of college her father hadn't found out about.

"I like the steps you taught me earlier," she said and moved forward through the crowd.

"So do I."

Her jeans were snug against her hips and thighs. Her short dark hair matched her spunky attitude that she clung to in spite of being drugged, kidnapped, shot at and meeting her parents' ghosts head-on over the past week.

Sexy wasn't a good enough description. Admiration didn't seem a strong enough word. Courageous even fell short.

"We're early right? Your friend George won't be here for a couple of minutes." She took hold of his hand, tugging him behind her to the dance floor. "I love this song."

Dancing. Not a problem. He recognized the words from Faith Hill's *This Kiss*. Jo's hips swayed to the music. More than one unattached man—and a couple on the arms of other women—took a second look as she passed by.

High heels instead of boots extended her legs and brought her lips closer to his when he turned her to face him. If he tasted her sweetness, he'd be swinging her off the dance floor, out the door and back to their motor home bedroom.

Levi needed to watch everyone and having his hind-side exposed without backup was completely against everything he'd been taught. But there were some other things he'd been taught as well. And a good dance was one of them.

He could try to justify it all he wanted. Plain fact was he *wanted* to dance with Jo.

Confidence. He could hear his dance instructor shouting across the room. Half the battle of leading a woman

backward in front of a couple of hundred people was the confidence that he didn't look like a dork.

"You really can dance," Jo said after he'd twirled her back into his arms.

"I'd hate to embarrass Mrs. Shapiro."

"A dance teacher? You took lessons?" She looked more surprised than finding out he was a native Texan.

"My aunt insisted."

"I don't know anything about you, Levi." She tipped her face up to look at him.

"I think you know plenty."

Before she dug in her spurs and wanted more of his secrets, the song ended and his excuse to keep his story for another time walked past them to the center bar. "George is in the dark denim shirt, third guy from the end."

"Rain check on the dancing?" she asked, looking at him through her long lashes. Disappointment was clearly written in her fake sad pout.

"You aren't escaping the full knowledge Mrs. Shapiro passed to me. I promise." He dropped a kiss on her forehead, unable to stop himself.

They made their way to George Lanning. Levi had met the FBI agent a couple of times while picking up a witness last year. Briefly. He didn't know much about the man except what his gut told him.

Good at his job. Dependable. Kept his mouth shut.

They shook hands, no introductions.

"Wanna keep this in the open? Or find a quiet corner?" Lanning asked, pointing to the back of the club.

He led them to a table, spoke to the waitress as if he knew her and ordered them a round of beers. "I guess you need a favor, Cooper, and I'm not going to like it much."

"I need information on a twenty-year-old murder."

George leaned his elbows on the table, dragging his

chair in a bit closer. Jo sat, seemingly relaxed, but her hands hugged her middle like it hurt again. He could tell she was nervous, even if the rest of the room couldn't.

"I'm assuming I don't want to know *why* you can't request the info through normal channels?"

"It's better if we skip that part."

"Anything to do with her?" Lanning cocked his head toward Jo who didn't change her expression.

"She was a witness to her mother's murder."

His answer must have surprised her. It surprised him to be so honest with a stranger. Lanning would know her real name, but not her current identity. It would all change when she went into protective custody anyway.

"What was she? Two?"

"Five," she corrected. "And I'm not a witness."

"When do you need things?"

"Yesterday."

"As always," Lanning answered. The waitress brought the long necks. He paid cash and winked.

"Cute. Is she why you come here on Thursdays?" Jo asked, tipping the bottle to her mouth.

Lanning smiled and took a long draught but didn't answer.

"Here's the case particulars." As they shook hands, Levi passed a note with the details he'd listed before leaving the motor home. "When do you think...?"

"Lunch tomorrow. Rock, paper or scissors?"

"Time for some rock."

"See you there at say, one? We'll miss the rush."

"That works."

Their last hope for a lead walked away with his beer, found his waitress empty-handed and twirled her before the bartender shouted at him to stop. "Can't a guy have

a little fun, Bobby?" he returned with a laugh like it was just another day.

For Lanning, it was just another day at work. As for Jo, it may never be a normal day again. Levi wanted a life for her. Wanted more than driving around in a motor home or wondering if she'd ever dance again.

"Rock, paper or scissors?" Jo asked.

"Possible restaurants. Rockfish or Paper Plates drive-through burgers."

"And the scissors?"

"It's a Japanese hibachi grill, lots of knives."

"Nice code." She tipped her bottle again. "Your friend's nice."

"Acquaintance, but he's a good guy." He finally took a swig of his own beer, letting down his guard for just a minute. "We'll know whatever the FBI knows tomorrow."

"And until then?"

"We wait." No one was shooting at them. No one seemed to be watching them. Well, not him. Jo was beautiful and still attracting attention.

"And how do you suggest we spend our time?"

"Well, I could show you a few more of Mrs. Shapiro's famous dance moves."

"Got any other famous moves you're ready to show off?"

"Only in the privacy of the motor home."

"Can't wait." Jo stood, offering her hand. "But since we paid to dance, how about another go? Cool dance floor."

Lanning moved to another group. No one seemed to be following him. Levi took her small hand into his, welcoming the chance to make her happy. Even if it had to end tomorrow.

GEORGE LANNING WATCHED Levi Cooper and Emaline Frasier—or Jo Atkins—dance around the center floor.

When they were out of sight, he set his earpiece and caught the chatter from the other agents located around Cowboys Red River.

He leaned on the bar, ignoring the couple as much as he could, following with his eyes and not his head. The other agents could handle trailing them so he enjoyed the last of his beer.

"That's it? You're walking away after a six-and-a-half-minute conversation?" his partner, Kendall Barlow, asked.

No—interrogated.

"Don't start. What else was I supposed to do? Chat them up to see how they were paying for their beer and ask 'Where are you staying?' He's good. Anything else and he would have been suspicious." He set his elbows on the bar, spying the flirty waitress he had a weekly dance with just to remind the bartenders he was there.

"I don't understand this assignment, George."

"We were asked to keep an eye on Marshal Cooper and the woman. Simple enough. We just need to find out where they're staying. The rest is need-to-know." *Look at them acting like there's not a major player out there with a hit man breathing down their necks.*

"I think they're sort of cute together. He's a pretty good dancer."

"He's taken."

"I can tell. Same as every woman in here who has one eye and half a brain."

"Surveillance is cutting into my dancing," he said with his feet tapping and ready to move. It was on the tip of his tongue to ask if she wanted to take a spin. Naw, she might read something into it.

"Rough job."

"Targets are headed toward the front." He heard another agent state through his earpiece.

Kendall pushed her stool away and followed Cooper and his charge to the exit. "Remember, there are enough of us here to find out where they're at without blowing our cover. Hang back," she stated the obvious to them all.

A couple of minutes later, as Lanning made his way to the parking lot, Kendall's voice laughed into his ear.

"You're not going to believe this, George, but it'll be super hard to lose sight of this getaway vehicle they're climbing into."

"What?" he asked.

"We found their hotel."

"Quit joking around, Barlow." George caught up with her, and she pointed. A motor home. "Find out where they're parking this thing."

George took the case info Cooper had palmed him, climbed into his truck and dialed his Agent in Charge. "I got it and you're not going to like it."

# Chapter Fourteen

No one paid attention to her with the good-looking men sitting at the table. It was actually fun watching the waitresses eyeing the federal agent as he'd come in the door. George Lanning looked like one hundred percent cowboy on his day off as much as he had dancing. Royal blue pick-up, scuffed boots, straw cowboy hat, T-shirt under a Western-cut suede jacket and a very nice-to-look-at pair of faded jeans.

But Jo was very satisfied with the muscles and the gorgeous man sitting next to her in his simple golf shirt. Her own "cowboy" protected her from the rest of the room, leaning forward if she did, then back when she rested against the booth. He'd done the same thing last night at the bar.

Maybe that's why she wasn't as apprehensive as she'd been for the past week? Or it could have everything to do with yesterday's relaxing afternoon, dancing last night and their nowhere-to-be morning with breakfast in bed. Oh, well, back to the nerve-racking conversation being dished up for lunch.

This meeting with George was comfortable and terrifying at the same time. They were tucked away in a corner of an Irving restaurant, hoping no one overheard their discussion of murder. With television screens on every wall

providing sports noise, it seemed unlikely, but they still spoke in whispers.

"A wife of a colleague discovered a back door into the Bureau during another case. I went to her for help. Jane knows her stuff. No reason to worry, it was the safest way and no one knows we were there."

Jo patted Levi's thigh when it stiffened beside hers. She could tell he wanted to shout at George for involving yet another person in their search. He didn't and under the table, laced his fingers through hers.

"You're certain no one detected anything and no one tailed you?" Levi asked.

George seemed confident enough he hadn't been followed, but she still caught herself looking around the room, scrutinizing the faces to see if any would morph into an anime cartoon. No tears or flashbacks this time. She tapped the table and kept her emotions in check while thinking of her mother's murderer.

"The file's been flagged. We found that someone began digging into Elaine Frasier's murder over a year ago."

"That's six months before the convenience store murder," Levi said in the low voice he'd been using for the entire conversation. "If they reopened the case, it would explain why the killer has waited so long to eliminate the only known witnesses."

"I still think it's a lot of trouble for them to flush us from hiding. It's a very slim chance I can remember a face from twenty years ago." Jo was surprised her voice wasn't ear-piercingly high with the uncertainty she felt. "Doesn't it make more sense that the investigation risked exposing them to prosecution?"

"Exactly." George drained his tea glass. Two waitresses picked up pitchers and raced to the table. One filled the glass and the other left her pitcher. "Thanks."

Jo buried her laugh and waited for them to leave. How could things seem so real, yet the situation was anything but? She'd fallen in love with a man who had hidden his identity from her. Made love to him before knowing if he had one living relative. She was still waiting to further that conversation. It seemed the more she tried to escape lies in her life, the more she was surrounded by them.

"Whatever they're trying to cover up, they're convinced it's worth killing to do so," George said.

"Can we assume that the man chasing us has a lot of influence? I mean, they knew when the case was reopened. Maybe they have a secret that needs to stay hidden," she added.

Levi had been very quiet. Listening, contemplating, watching.

"Makes sense," he finally said. "They're worried about something that's still relevant to whoever would have been prosecuted by the DoJ. And Jo's the only witness left to eliminate."

The food arrived, everyone was quiet. Somehow the entire restaurant went quiet, too. She knew what Levi said was true, but his matter-of-fact statement for some reason chilled her to the bone.

"I'm willing to help on this, Cooper, official capacity or not," George said, fork in his hand ready to dig into his salmon.

"You've done enough, Lanning. The Department of Justice and Marshals Service don't consider this a case—"

"Don't mention it. I sort of like your girl here."

*His girl?*

Levi released her hand with a squeeze. Was she Levi's girl? At least until he sent her off to WITSEC for a new life. Oh yes, that's exactly what that look of his meant.

Definitely a conversation they'd need to repeat soon. He needed to accept she wasn't headed to WITSEC.

"Did you see anything in the file? I've been over it a hundred times in the past four years. Nothing seemed out of the ordinary and both agencies seemed to have covered all aspects of the case."

"The list of clients," she said, jumping back into the conversation. "Most listed their occupations as savings and loans officers in the '80s. A lot of their banks failed."

"I didn't know you'd looked at the file." Levi sat back, seemingly in no hurry to eat the fried catfish on his plate.

"That's an angle the original investigation followed. It didn't pan out," George stated. "I can find out what's happened to those clients over the past twenty years. It might just be the substantial lead we need."

Levi smiled at her, she couldn't decipher why. "The client with the most to lose is our guy." Then he turned to his plate of food. "It always comes back to money."

IT TOOK SEVERAL minutes to walk across the busy intersection and to the other end of the strip mall which included a busy grocery store. They quickly crossed over the highway into a subdivision, taking side streets in case they were followed. Jo had been in the back of the motor home and came to the front when they slowed for a school zone.

"Look. Normal people." She laughed at Levi before belting herself into the passenger seat.

"What do you mean?"

He hadn't heard her laugh in a long while. Not a carefree laugh. Since their first kiss and subsequent years in Georgia, she'd been guarded. Watching what she said and limiting any time alone with him if her father had left the room.

It was good to hear her laugh.

"They're walking their kids home from school. Stopping

at the swings in the park. Discussing what they learned in class today. You know, normal. Wondering what's for dinner is their current, most pressing problem."

"That's the life you want?"

"Someday," she answered with a longing sigh.

"You sound like it's a faraway dream. It's right around the corner." He drove and noticed her laughter and smiles had stopped. Replaced by the are-you-serious face. A guaranteed warning not to pursue his line of questioning. But he did anyway. "What's that look for?"

"Are you kidding? It's a pipe dream."

"We're close to finding the evidence. When we do, the Department of Justice will offer you protection and you won't feel like this any longer." He patted her arm, wanting her fingers back in his hand to reassure her. Didn't happen. She yanked away, popped her seat belt open and darted out of his reach.

"Just how do you think I feel, Levi? Remind me again what happens in your world when the DoJ offers me *protection?*"

He could see her in the corner of his eye, swaying with the motions of the motor home, braced against the cabinets lining the wall. "Come back and put your seat belt on, Jo. You're making me nervous."

"Seriously? That's how you're going to avoid this conversation?"

"I'm not certain what conversation we're actually having."

She moved to the rear and slammed the door to the bedroom. He paid closer attention to their surroundings, parking in their assigned spot. He jumped out, not allowing himself to go to Jo. If he did, he'd kiss her until she had hope again.

That's what he'd seen…hopelessness.

"You think my life's going to be fine," Jo said behind him. She'd left the other side of the trailer and he hadn't heard her round the corner. "Another marshal will take me into custody, whisk me off, protect me, give me a new identity. You want me to fall in love, have a family and lie every single day about who I am. Perhaps putting them in danger, looking over my shoulder, waiting for a stinking *Rainbow Man* to come and take them all from me."

That wasn't what he wanted. He couldn't turn and face her. The thought of never seeing her again had him paralyzed. Through the side-view mirror he could see her hugging her middle, tears streaking her beautiful cheeks.

"I refuse to lie to the people I love, Levi. I simply can't do it. So yes, taking a walk home from school or swinging my kids in the park…it's just a dream that will never happen."

The urge to turn and pull her into his arms was so great he stuck his hands in his jeans pockets to stop himself. He felt a sharp stab. Not just figuratively. The physical ache was there, working its way from his closed throat which had cut off the words of comfort already in his head.

He couldn't tell her it would be different. Experience told him she was right.

"Let's get through the rest of this mess," she cried. "I'm willing to pay whatever the price to find my parents' murderer."

The pain moved lower, deeper. Alarm. Fright.

"Whatever dreams I had are gone. Thanks for the reality check." She took a couple of steps backward, made eye contact in the mirror as if she'd known all along he'd been watching her there, turned and walked away.

Panic. She was gone. He couldn't do it…*Let her go.*

He had to or she'd never be safe.

*She'll never be happy. She just told you she wouldn't.*

What other choice was there? He had a life protecting others. Or could choose a life where she didn't have to lie again. First they had to find a murderer.

A LIFE WITHOUT Levi. A life without love versus a life without lies.

Who was she? Jolene Atkins or Emaline Frasier?

Some people might be thrilled starting over and leaving everything behind. Not her. She didn't care what her name was or where she would live, or even what she did for a living. That wasn't the point.

Her life had been decided by the Marshals Service and her father. What she knew. When she knew. Or even how much she knew. All carefully weighed decisions so she'd never understand the complete truth. She hated waiting to discover what her fate would be. When would she take the driver's seat of her own life?

If she wanted to control her fate, then it was time to take responsibility.

The life she wanted began now.

Her hand had been on the open motor home door while the thoughts spun through her head. Instead of entering the confined space again, she walked to the park's office to call a cab, setting an idea into motion that she wouldn't be able to stop.

*No turning back.*

Her actions may be interpreted as too stupid to live but there wasn't another choice. If she did come through to the other side, Levi would certainly kill her. This crazy cat-and-mouse game would be done. Over. Finished.

Jo assumed George Lanning was a good FBI Agent. He may actually be able to find a connection or a lead. But whoever this mysterious client was, they'd had twenty

years to hide any evidence. Twenty years to become even more powerful.

Whoever they were, they'd killed both her parents to cover up their secret.

The fastest way to find her mother's client was to let them find her. When they did, she'd end it. She had to end this. No more sacrifices to keep her safe.

No more running.

Levi would never agree.

*Then Levi couldn't know until it was too late.*

## Chapter Fifteen

Jolene couldn't leave without a goodbye. She'd given herself plenty of time to get away from Levi. The cab would be at the office in half an hour. One last meal, one last moment of pretending to be happy.

One last opportunity to change her mind.

No, she was in control.

She would have been frozen from the cold if she'd been sitting outside as long as Levi. Dinner wasn't anything spectacular but it was on the table when she called him inside.

"I think we should talk, Jo." He sat with a defeated plop. "George called."

"Eat." She joined him. *Don't lose your resolve.* "Did he come up with a short list of potential people?"

"He did, but more importantly, he's got a place you can stay while I check these people out."

"And if I don't want to hide?" She choked down a bite of the spaghetti.

"It's not hiding. It's saving your life. We'll be stirring up God knows what and—"

"And you can't do your job if I'm around. Got it. Eat."

"It's not that simple."

"You've made it very easy to understand." He was send-

ing her away. FBI or Marshals Service, he was sending her away. "So this is goodbye. When will they be here?"

His way meant it was unlikely she'd ever see him again. Especially if he was successful and found the evidence implicating one of her mother's clients. *Twenty-five minutes until her cab arrived.* Her way was dangerous, but in her limited experience, worth the risk.

"George is picking you up at eight." He poked his fork into the noodles, not putting any between his lips. "It's not goodbye. I need to know you're safe, dammit. This wasn't an easy decision."

"Of course it wasn't." She ate, not tasting anything. She forced the calories down, finishing her plate. If her plan was successful, they'd see each other later. "But then, I wouldn't know because you made it without me. Excuse me, I'm going to pack my toothbrush."

"Jo…" he called as if she had no right to her feelings. He snagged her arm, tilting his head at the last minute to look at her. "It's for the best."

"I know you believe that." She looked at his hand and he released her. "There's something you should know."

He turned to her, hands rubbing up and down his jeans. It was so hard not to push him against the bench seat and kiss him until he made love to her. But it was difficult enough to stick to her plan just being in the same room with him. If she touched him, would she be able to walk out the door?

*You're in control. He can't make life-changing decisions for you.*

"What?" he asked.

"I want to thank you for saving my life, Levi."

"We'll have plenty of time to talk about that later."

"We may not." The desire to stay with him or even wait for him at wherever he wanted to send her, made her hesi-

tate. *Stay strong.* "I've appreciated everything you've done even if I didn't always seem grateful."

"Jo, I'm the reason you're in this mess. I'm the reason you've nearly been killed and if I'd been doing my job—"

"Which I hope you get back. I know how important it is to you."

He stood. "You really are saying goodbye." He took her hands, indicating he wanted to pull her into an embrace, but she stood firm, remaining an arm's length away. "This is only temporary."

"You never know what'll happen." She shook off his touch again, unsure if she'd be able to hide her emotion another fifteen minutes.

"I should have gotten you to safety from the beginning. If I had I wouldn't have been suspended. Don't you see, Jo? This is the only way to find the murderer."

"I agree." *This is the only way.*

Unable to face him anymore, she ran across the small space to the bedroom, hoping he'd wait for Agent Lanning outside. A few minutes later and she felt the motor home shift and listened for the door to close. She peeked out the window and watched him cross to the table he'd been sitting on before.

"I know you're going to be mad, Levi. But it's time for this damsel in distress to take charge. I just hope you find my clues and can rescue me one last time."

LEVI ENTERED THE motor home with a bit of apprehension. He'd struggled with the decision to send her with Lanning. The last thing he wanted was to be separated after finally admitting to himself how much he cared. Putting her safety into someone else's hands went against his makeup. It's what he did—protect people.

In this case, it was the right thing to do. He would think

clearer knowing she wasn't in danger. But the look of hurt and betrayal on Jo's face had changed his mind—twice. He'd had the cell in his hand both times dialing Lanning to call it off. Each time he walked himself through almost losing her on the train, remembering the dead woman who looked like Jo.

"Jo?"

She'd be safe with Lanning's friends.

"I thought you said she was ready to go." Lanning had followed.

"She's gone. Must have left out the driver's door, but there's nowhere for her to go."

"Man, I think you got that wrong. There's an entire city of places out there for her. What are you doing?"

"Calling the stupid burner she has."

The ring was screaming through the silence as they waited for someone to pick up.

Lanning followed the noise back to the passenger seat. "She's gone."

"She'll be back." She had to be back.

"Not according to this." Lanning held a piece of notebook paper. "'Glad you found this, Marshal,'" Lanning read aloud. "'I've set my own plan in motion which involves your FBI friends tracking my location through my cell. For your convenience I've activated the GPS.' That's one smart girlfriend you've got Cooper."

"Smart? She knows how the men tracked her in St. Louis. She's just told the murderer where she's at. Is there any more? Like what she actually has planned?"

Levi let Lanning continue as he looked in the cabinet where they'd stored his duffel and the dog statues.

"'I meant what I said this afternoon,'" Lanning read, "'I'm willing to do whatever it takes to find my mother's client. This is the fastest way. Don't be late.'"

"She took the pup. The statue that matched this." He held the carved dog that Joseph had given him. "Let's go."

"She's using herself as bait?" Lanning asked. "Why didn't she just tell us where she was headed?"

"She wants the murderer to find her first. We can't let that happen." He had his hand on the door, pulling it open when Lanning slammed it shut.

"Hold on. She wants you to turn on your cell and expect a call."

"We aren't waiting here for those vultures to demand the evidence."

"No. We're not. But I need to make a call, find out where we need to go, alert my team. We don't know what direction she went. Think this through." Lanning shoved him back to the bench seat. "Look over the short list. See if anything rings a bell. There are some powerful people with a lot to lose."

"I blame myself. I should have talked this through with her, got her to see it my way."

"Maybe. Maybe not. You know the drill, man. We can't second-guess everything before now. Gotta focus."

Levi didn't respond. Lanning dialed his cell, alerting the FBI and requesting the Bureau to pinpoint Jo's cell.

"Plano. Yeah. Got it. I want a unit there ASAP." Lanning put his cell in his shirt pocket and opened the door. "What are you waiting on? She used her credit card this afternoon to check into a hotel."

"That's impossible. She was here with me the entire time."

"Obviously not the entire time," Lanning said. "You can beat yourself up in the truck. It's possible Frasier's client already knows where she's at." He headed out the door, letting it slam behind him.

Stunned. At a loss for words. He couldn't think. Couldn't

move. Out of every scenario he'd gone through this afternoon, he hadn't thought of this. He'd never considered that Jo might actually die.

He could have lived with himself if he'd sent her away to keep her safe. Survive. Hell, the possibility of actually breaking the rules and finding her in the WITSEC program sometime in the future had even entered his mind.

But not her dead. He wouldn't let that happen. He still held the dog Joseph had given him. He hated to destroy it, but there wasn't time for an X-ray. Grabbing a steak knife from the drawer, he began sawing at the head.

He used his frustration to hack. The anger he felt blocked his ability to reason logically and use his training. How could the woman he love leave him and put herself at risk?

*Love? Yeah, my timing sucks.*

The possibility of losing Jo and never telling her, well...

"Not happening."

"Um, Cooper?" Lanning stuck his head inside, looking as headless as the small statue in his hands. "Crafts?"

"There must have been a seam where Atkins reattached the head. He gave this to Jo. We were having it X-rayed tomorrow." He looked inside the hollow body and removed a slip of paper. "I'm going to need to talk with your best researcher."

"'Bout time you caught a break."

"Nobody but your guy and the two of us knows these. We're not taking any chances. It's the only leverage we'll have to get her back."

Levi shoved the paper deep in his pocket and followed Lanning to the truck. *I love you, Jo, and you better damn well stay alive!*

# Chapter Sixteen

TEXT MESSAGE: Blocked Sender 8:02 P.M.
The girl will be brought to you at the arranged location.
Don't screw this up.

JOLENE PROPPED THE door to the hotel room open and sat in the chair, waiting, phone in hand, finger ready to record whoever walked inside.

Her plan had seemed so simple when she'd called the taxi. First: reserve the room using her credit card to alert the person tracking her. Second: get to the hotel, turn the cell on to make it even easier to locate her. And third: wait for the murderer to show up. Assuming they still wanted her alive, she'd convince them to take her to the real person in charge before she divulged where the evidence was located. She'd lie about the significance of the matching carved statue and say it was in a Colorado safe deposit box.

"What an idiotic plan," she whispered to herself. "They'd be better off killing me right here."

*Then leave.*

Even though she didn't share her plan with him, she knew Levi would find her. She watched the door, afraid to move from her spot and be taken by surprise.

What would she do if Levi and his FBI friends showed up before the men chasing her? Convince them this was

the only option to flush out the person who ordered the murders. Would they let her stay? She didn't know who she hoped would arrive first. Levi would surely kill her either way.

"Well, isn't this an interesting change of events." Sadie Colter was dressed in slacks and a business shirt, looking professional with her designer coat draped over her arm. "Face-to-face once again. You've given us quite a chase, Ms. Frasier."

The gun pointed straight at Jo let her know exactly whose side her former sitter was on.

"You look surprised. Didn't you send for me? I believe I even arrived before you. I've been watching to see if your fed friends showed up."

Gone was the bleached blond hair, obnoxious red lipstick and nails. She meandered into the room, looking around, unconcerned about concealing her face. She quietly let the door click shut and flipped the lock. "I'm going to search you to make sure you aren't wired. Can't have that ruin all the fun."

The woman patted her through her clothing, looked at several obvious places around the room and seemed satisfied there weren't any listening devices. She searched Jo's coat lying on the bed and found the dog, placing it in her own coat pocket.

"So you cleaned it up. Good job, Emmy."

*What am I doing?* She tapped the record button on the phone still in her hand. "You were my babysitter, LuLu. I recognized you at my old house."

"You know, I thought you might be catching on towards the end." She popped her gum, slipping into the Sadie Colter accent and persona. "I told them leaving the house that way was a bit much, kinda sick, you know? I have to say, that psychic bit was hilarious. Well done."

"You knew who I was the entire time?"

"Oh, honey. They've been waiting for you to come back. Your dad was a surprise. I really thought he was dead. But you? Leaving you alive was a mistake."

"You were there when my mother was murdered?"

"Who do you think unlocked the door? Of course they didn't know I was there." Quickly, she stood straight, and gestured with the gun to stand. "You always were a smart child. Too bad your dad sniffed around. I did like him."

"Did you kill my father, too?"

The horrible woman just raised her thin eyebrows. "We should go. I'm sure your Marshal Cooper will be here shortly. By the way, he's a cutie to watch—even from a distance. Bet you had some fun exploring every inch of that tall hunk."

"I came alone. He doesn't know." *But I hope he's on his way.*

"If that's the truth, Emmy, honey," she pouted, "then I'm afraid you don't have much bargaining power. Put your phone on the table. You won't be needing it any time soon."

Jo set the phone on the dresser. She'd called her Emmy. Strange that there wasn't a glimmer of memory attached to the name.

Should she want to hurt this woman who had confessed to opening the door for the murderers? Did her look implicate her in the murder of her father? Surely they'd still be able to prosecute based on the recorded conversation. It didn't matter. Finding her mother's client…the person who ordered LuLu to spy on them. That was her goal.

Everything was on the line.

"Did my father recognize you? Is that why you killed him?" Jo walked past her, leaving the phone on the dresser, still recording the conversation…hopefully. "Where are you taking me? Who are you really?"

"I trust you can keep your mouth shut as we leave. You know the drill, right?" LuLu ignored her questions. "I'll shoot you, but I have several other bullets and I'm a fairly good shot. A lot of innocent people will die. And you care about that, don't you?"

Of course she didn't want anyone else to get hurt. And her ultimate goal was to find her mother's client. Not to escape…yet.

LuLu—or whoever she was—hid behind a scarf, large sunglasses and her coat. Once out the room door, she grabbed Jo's elbow, curling sharp nails into the soft skin Levi had brought to life with his kisses just that morning. The gun was shoved into her ribs, hidden by Jo's jacket.

The woman didn't answer her questions. They walked silently, but at a steady pace to the elevators. It would be useless to talk anyway. She could only hope that the hotel manager remembered what she'd asked him to do.

LEVI SWUNG OPEN the door and jumped from the truck before Lanning threw the vehicle into Park behind the Plano squad car. He was through the hotel's automatic doors and waved toward the counter. "Where is she?"

"The manager says she left less than fifteen minutes ago with this woman." The cop handed him a picture.

"Sadie Colter. Now a brunette, but I recognize her under the glasses. Definitely the woman known as LuLu from Jo's past." How the heck was she connected to all this? One of Frasier's clients? A plant in the house?

"How did you know to take a picture and call the police?" Lanning asked the manager.

"Ms. Atkins came to me and explained that you would need a picture of the person she'd be leaving with. I don't like the idea of my hotel being used for a sting operation. This is very disruptive. I hope this is what you wanted. It

was clearly a woman who came through the lobby with her. FBI or police, I swear—"

"Just tell us what Jolene said," Levi interrupted the man. They were losing time.

"She told us to give the information regarding the vehicle and physical description to the police as soon as she'd gone. I was surprised when this officer showed up minutes after we called."

"Is that it?"

"I still don't think it's right to put this type of responsibility..."

Levi walked away, pulling the agent behind him.

Lanning stopped him just outside the door. "I'm saying this again, Cooper, your girl's pretty dang smart."

"And if we don't find her, she'll be pretty dang dead when they discover she doesn't know anything."

"Give Russell some time. He's digging through twenty years of information to find our likely candidates. We know more than they think we know." He slapped Levi's shoulder. "I'm going to check the room. You coming?"

They rode the elevator and verbalized the laundry list of standard operating procedures: cell phone trace, vehicle location, how to handle the exchange, not to be too cocky on the phone with the middle man.

Levi listened. For once, wanting someone to tell him exactly what to do. If something happened then he could blame someone else. Naw, no matter what, he would be solely responsible. Should he use Lanning or go at this alone?

*Alone. Trust his gut. No rules.*

Every other thought had him returning to why Jo had left him. She'd clearly made the decision while he'd been talking to Lanning that afternoon, giving whoever LuLu worked for enough time to find her at this hotel.

Knowing that he couldn't keep her safe, wondering what was best had been making him question himself. He thought that arranging for the FBI to take over her protective custody would drive him crazy wondering if she was safe. He'd even toyed with the idea of taking off in that motor home and never looking back.

But this...the possibility that Jo was already dead ate away at his insides. If she were...Well, he understood what a better half meant now. His would be gone forever.

"They're ready with the trace." One of Lanning's team informed them when the elevator doors opened. "Everything's set in the room. No prints. No disturbance. No one heard a thing. Nothing in the room except Ms. Atkins's cell."

"Pull the records," Lanning said, handing the phone off to a woman who entered after them. "Look through its history."

Levi was good with faces. He'd seen this one before. He moved out of the way, trying to place her. "Who's the blonde?" he asked one of the men who'd come up with them.

"Special Agent Barlow, just transferred from Austin or San Antonio."

Levi knew he'd seen her. Somewhere here in Dallas. Recently. Then it hit him. New boots, dark jeans, tan shirt. She'd stood right next to the FBI agent while at the bar. Lanning.

They'd been set-up.

The jerk he'd trusted to help Jolene walked from the room into the hallway. Levi followed, spinning him around. He grabbed Lanning's collar just as Lanning crunched his wrists in a death grip.

"Where is she?"

# Chapter Seventeen

"Who brought you in?" Levi shouted, yanking on Lanning's collar in spite of the agent's bruising grasp.

"I don't let many men get away with messing up my shirt." Lanning warned a cop off with a look. "How did you know?"

"Blondie was at the bar with you last night, followed us outside." As much as Levi wanted to knock Lanning flat on his butt, he released him with a push and took a step away. "You played me."

"It wasn't my call. Your guy talked to my guy. We were to apprise them if you contacted us. I followed orders." He acted like it was no big deal and Levi would understand.

The old Levi—the go-to guy at the Denver office—he would have understood. The new man standing in a Plano hotel crazy to find the one woman he'd fallen in love with…*That* guy wanted to crash some heads together. Levi walked to the end of the hall, dialing a number he'd known for eight years.

"Good evening, Cooper." Sherry Peachtree's voice needed no identification.

"Did you want to talk to me?"

"Not particularly," she stated bluntly. "How long did you think you could continue to run an operation while you're suspended? You asked for favors, Levi. If you'll

remember, I'm the one that introduced you to those men who could have lost their jobs helping you."

"I'm done."

"Are you asking or telling? I can't differentiate by your tone."

This time it was easier to remain silent. The job wasn't the most important thing in his life. Part of him would always be a marshal. The better part would be lost without Jo.

"Ah, so I have your attention. Your non-witness has unwittingly come up with a half-decent plan that might actually flush out the murderer of our men, resolving this mystery."

A long pause. He didn't like it, but he kept silent. He needed both agencies to find Jo. "What plan?"

"Lord have mercy, Cooper. I thought you were up to speed. Jolene Atkins purchased a GPS locater and sent the tracking information to her phone. The Bureau hasn't found her yet. We're assuming she hasn't turned it on."

*She might already be dead?*

His mouth went all sorts of dry, choked. He couldn't get his teeth unhinged to speak. Whatever it was, he couldn't listen any longer, either. Suddenly, Lanning was in front of him, taking the phone from his hand.

"Yes ma'am. Got it. Will do." The agent clicked the end call button and tossed the phone to him.

"She's dead." That staggering pain throughout his body was back. "You know the only reason she wouldn't have the tracker on is if she's dead."

"Or it's not working. Or they destroyed it. Or she's waiting. Pull yourself together, man. They'll be calling and you need to be ready. We got your back."

They waited in the hotel room. He didn't pay attention to the time. Men and women were busy around him and

he was useless, ordered to stay put. He could only think about his mistakes and pray Jolene was alive. Then his cell buzzed. Lanning and his techs nodded.

"Cooper."

"You know we have the woman," a distorted mechanical-sounding voice said. "You have something else we want."

"Where and when?" He rubbed the back of his neck, debating what he should do. They wouldn't give Jo back. Not alive. And the FBI wouldn't share the evidence *if* they found any. He had to do things his way or she was dead.

The tech gave the sign to stretch out the call.

"One hour. We'll call—"

"You have a problem," he interrupted. "I don't deal with middle men."

"Marshal, think about Ms. Frasier's health."

Lanning shook his head, mouthing "don't."

"Alone. Top dog or no meet."

"What are you doing?" Lanning whispered through gritted teeth.

Levi set the phone away from him, praying to God he knew the answer. Concentrating on making his voice as flat and unemotional as possible, he answered, "Miller and Phillips. I have what you want and you have what's mine."

"One hour. Ditch the feds."

The line disconnected. The tech shook his head.

"What did you just do?" Lanning looked like he would blow a gasket.

"I gave us time to form a workable plan and hopefully time for Jolene to turn on the GPS. Did you have something better?"

"We're not turning over Frasier's evidence."

"What evidence? No one's found a thing. Have you?" Was Lanning lying to him again? Even if he had, he wouldn't give it to him. The DoJ had waited twenty years.

"You claimed—"

"Talk. It's what they expected and gave us time. That's all I need to save her."

"We don't have any information to share. I'll need your phone."

Levi handed the man his only connection to Jo. It was either that or be tackled to the ground making a run for it. "You've handed her a death sentence."

Lanning patted his shoulder then drew him in close. "Levi, you know I like Jo. But orders are orders. Sorry, man. Officer, make sure he stays close."

*Orders were orders.*

A set of pickup keys slipped into his jacket pocket was about as direct an order as he'd received. The police officer standing nearby stood a bit straighter, physically letting him know he'd accepted his own instructions.

Levi needed a hint, something to fake the information the murderers wanted. As soon as he knew what the paper inside the statue meant, he'd leave.

He'd have a head start. A chance.

TEXT MESSAGE: Blocked Sender 8:28 P.M.
You know what to do. No loose ends.

JO HAD HER bases covered. Or so she'd thought. Her hands were behind her back, handcuffed, crunched in the floorboard of the backseat. LuLu turned the radio on and sang with an off-pitch screech.

Simple enough. Let herself be captured and tracked to her mother's client. Levi finds her at the last minute, rescues her and they capture the bad guy. She'd seen it a hundred times in the movies.

*Right, and they climbed out windows of speeding trains, too!* Levi's voice echoed in her ear.

The hotel manager and desk clerk had agreed to help by giving the information to the police. She was surprised when LuLu hadn't bothered to hide her face from hotel cameras. She'd even parked in the drop-off zone. It didn't make sense. If she'd been attempting to kidnap her and shoot Levi all this time, then why wasn't she more worried about hiding her identity?

Something was terribly wrong.

The murderer had been one step ahead of them until they'd purchased the motor home. What had made her think she could outsmart them with this pathetic plan? There was a reason she'd been letting Levi take charge. He was a U.S. Marshal with tons of experience. Even with a few hiccups, he knew what he was doing. Her plan was full of flaws and she'd deliberately placed herself in danger.

Two or three miles from the hotel, they switched cars. "Stolen?" she asked, awkwardly caught on the floor between the seats, with her feet going to sleep under her.

"What makes you say that? Don't I look like the motherly type?" LuLu referred to the child booster in the back-seat.

"The car was in an empty lot, unlocked, keys under the floor mat. You even had to adjust the seat."

"You are smart. But not smart enough to realize who I am and why everyone wants you dead."

"I hope to find out and put you in jail."

"Sister, you're barking up the wrong tree. These people aren't going to tell you why they killed your mother. She's not the only one they've taken out along the way." She cleared her throat and drove. "You're so naïve."

"You could get out. You know witness protection works."

"That would imply I actually want out." She laughed, sounding a little hysterical and a lot scared. "I'm really

sorry it came to this, Emmy. Why couldn't you walk away?"

*No. No. No. Ask her what she means.*

"Did you…" *Calmly.* "Did you use to babysit me and call me Emmy?"

"Everyone called you Emmy. Emaline was so, well, pretentious. And yes, I watched you for your mom. And before you ask anything else, this isn't a good conversation to have. You're not going to like the answers."

*She* wasn't Emmy. That little girl no longer existed. Weird that in the midst of a terrifying car ride to who knew where, she'd make a breakthrough about her identity. She was Jolene Atkins and she knew who her father had been. She wished she'd trusted Levi just a little more.

"Of course I want to know the truth."

"Girlie, I know you're searching a list of clients that would have reason to kill your mother. I'm not stupid."

"And you don't think I want to know the real reason my parents died?"

"Will it make the hurt go away? No."

*No, the hurt won't go away.* "I still need to learn what happened. That's why I'm here."

"I know I shouldn't. I'm not supposed to talk with you at all."

Jo remained quiet. She didn't know how to encourage this woman to put herself in danger. She didn't know how much time remained before she'd be face-to-face with her parents' murderer. She didn't believe that the talkative LuLu had actually wielded the knife or pulled the trigger.

"Sorry to tell you this, hon. Your mother was neck-deep in the quicksand that would bring down some very influential people. Still could. She made some powerful enemies. You don't ever walk away from people like that. You only get carried out in a body bag."

"My mother couldn't have known she was doing business with dangerous people. My father wouldn't—There's no way."

"They didn't know until it was too late. And it looks like Elaine never told him. Otherwise, the cops would be screaming down our necks instead of you digging into all this mess."

"Why did you kill her?"

"Killed or be killed, honey. It's a simple rule to live by. Now shut up. I've talked way too much."

"Can you tell me what they were trying to hide?" Yes, she really wanted to know. She'd been in the dark much too long.

"Let's just say they made lots of money and won't go to jail. They're the people everyone talks about getting away with whatever 'it' is and your mother helped them do it legally."

It didn't matter that LuLu wanted her to be quiet. Jo wouldn't listen to her trash. "You're wrong. I may not know much about my mother, but I know my father and he wouldn't have been with the person you're describing."

LuLu may only know the version of the story *the client* wanted her to have. The enemy wasn't her mom. Anger mixed with the fright of the unknown around her. She had to discover the truth. And would live with whatever happened.

Maybe the quiet, sedate life was the way to go after all. No traveling in the motor home. All she needed was a quiet backyard where she could watch amazing sunsets with Levi.

*Levi. Find the phone.*

Jo had no clue where they were in Dallas. It didn't matter as long as Levi could find her.

They stopped. The small car had bucket seats and if

she stretched, she could see LuLu's brown hair and arm as she unbuckled. A moment later, the door was opened and a shot split the silence. LuLu slumped across the emergency brake.

*Oh, my God!*

The door closest to her head opened, the evening breeze cooled her hot skin. Jo bit her bottom lip to keep from screaming. Shock kept her immobile, silent. And fear kept her eyes tightly shut waiting for the second shot.

"No." She couldn't believe LuLu was dead. But she was. Very dead. And if Levi or the FBI had trouble tracking where she was, she would be joining her former babysitter.

Jo didn't even know her real name.

Without speaking, the shooter removed a small electronic device from under the seat. He must have listened to their conversation.

Continuing his silence, he taped her mouth shut, hauled her from the floorboards. Smiling all the while like Hannibal Lector—a lecherous, evil tilt to his lips proved he'd enjoyed the murder he'd just committed.

*He's not wearing a mask. Bad sign, right?*

The guy was the same build as the man who had grabbed her at the hotel, old enough to have murdered her mother, somewhere in his late forties. He certainly had the actions of a cold-blooded murderer. The way he'd shot LuLu was definitely heartless. He wasn't Japanese or had any resemblance to the anime character in her head. And he certainly didn't have blue or green straw-like hair.

Jo caught the shadow of another person at the wheel. As dark and sinister as the person at her back. Without a word, he shoved her into a food-service panel van. They left LuLu's body in the stolen car. No questions. No demands. Allowing her frightened feelings to run rampant.

Her shoulders were already aching from their awkward

position. There were no seats, no windows, no access to the driver. She'd definitely seen too many movies and murders on television. Vans were never a good sign.

LuLu had been right when she'd told her she didn't understand these people. She'd called her naïve. Her plan—or lack of a real plan—was going to get her killed. The cuffs were cutting into her wrists.

If they'd just get to where they were going then she'd be able to activate the GPS. She'd imagined they'd search her for electronics and hadn't wanted to take a chance turning it on until the last minute.

*Find the phone, Levi. Please find me.*

## Chapter Eighteen

"Okay, glad this is voicemail. I know you're angry and probably getting angrier. But I need you to know that I thought this through. Just find me and it'll be over. Then a *normal* life. Right? Before this thing cuts me off, I bought a GPS car locator. The information is in a note on my phone. I cut a hole in my shoe big enough to hold it. Hopefully they won't find it before you find me." A pause. "I know you'll find me."

Jo's voice did nothing to help him breathe easier.

The tech returned his phone and asked him to go through the messages, verifying he knew all the senders. Levi had plugged through them all anxious to hear Jo's voice and explanation. He'd listened several times trying to decipher a hidden meaning. There wasn't any.

No desperation. Maybe a spasm of jitters. Unfounded confidence in his abilities. He didn't have the expertise or equipment necessary to track Jo. If Lanning hadn't been involved before, Levi would have asked now. His new "best friend" joined him in the hall, looking at his notes, a bit of surprise on his face that Levi still stood in the same spot.

"LeeAnn Wright, also known as LuAnn Harper or Lisa Tucker. Jo's LuLu is a frequent flier with the law. Just skirts the dark side far enough not to get any hard time.

A long list of known associates." Lanning shook his head and answered his phone.

Levi knew what that look meant. He'd used it enough in his line of work. "A list long enough that it's useless. We don't have time or the manpower to go through it."

Lanning dropped his phone back in his pocket. "Worse. Wright was just found shot to death."

"What are we waiting on?"

"A phone call telling you where to go. There's nothing we can do at the crime scene except get sidetracked."

"We're doing nothing here. They might miss clues Jo has left. I can't just sit here like a useless—" Levi crunched an empty water bottle and caught himself before slamming it down the hall. He'd been purposefully calm for half an hour. The officer had relaxed. One sliver of information and he could search for Jo himself.

"We still have twenty-three minutes before he's supposed to call." Lanning turned to the men inside the room. "What have you got on the names and dates? Anything you've found, I need it now."

Levi followed Lanning to the doorway, entering the room slowly, not wanting anyone to realize he shouldn't be there.

"I can't find any connection," someone sitting in front of a screen said.

"What happened in February 1988 with the savings and loan crisis in Texas?" Levi asked. "Frasier's main clients were S and L trustees or owners. Concentrate on Texas."

"New regs, a bailout, fifty percent office vacancy and real estate prices collapse," the tech said.

"Money," Levi and Lanning said together.

Lanning lifted a hand to stop the agent who made a move to escort Levi back to the hall.

"What does this have to do with now?" Levi asked.

"I can cross-reference…"

"It happened again. We're calling it the housing crisis, but it's basically the same. Someone wants to make certain their part of it stays hidden." Barlow moved closer to the group. "Frasier hid the evidence."

Levi sided up to Jo's phone, activated the screen and in between the heated discussion on possible theories, he managed to get the GPS code from the note section.

"No one with these names was involved publicly with that crisis. There's nothing I can locate in the database."

"Miller February 1988 and Phillips March 1988," Levi repeated. "What are we not seeing? What did Frasier stumble across?" He returned to lean on the doorframe, keeping an eye on the cop who was supposed to be keeping an eye on him.

"If you go back to the file, notes from the original investigation said Frasier's records were boxed," Barlow said.

"Yes, but they've all been microfilmed by the DoJ."

"Don't you see? Her office was switching to digital in the nineties," Barlow interrupted. "Where could she have hidden paper files?"

"Wendell Miller and Frank Phillips died eight days apart, sir. Miller was a vice president at a failed S and L and Phillips was an appraiser. I haven't found a connection to the Frasier family."

"With the exception that they died less than a week later," Levi pointed out.

"That's too close to be coincidental. A banker, an appraiser and an attorney who specialized in realty," Lanning said. "Find the common denominator and make it fast."

Levi had what he needed. Names. A hint of what might have happened. Something to mislead the kidnappers for an exchange.

While everyone in the room was excitedly throwing

out theories, he glanced over his shoulder and the cop was talking at the end of the hall. Levi stepped the opposite direction, easing himself around another corner to an emergency exit.

A flight of stairs and a side door. Lanning's truck.

They could follow, but he had his head start.

His phone rang.

"Cooper."

An address and time were given by the distorted voice. The meeting place wouldn't matter if Jo activated the GPS. When she did, he could take them by surprise by intercepting her. "Come on, Jo. Turn on your rescue."

TEXT MESSAGE: Send Anonymously 9:14 P.M.
I have the girl, but there is a problem. At arranged meeting place.

TEXT MESSAGE: Blocked Sender 9:17 P.M.
I'll be downstairs momentarily.

THEY'D REMOVED JOLENE'S coat and already taken her dad's carving. The frightening men had placed headphones over her ears. The thundering music had given her an obnoxious headache. She didn't know how long she'd been in the smelly van. A bit of fresh air entered occasionally when the driver took a look inside.

Since her hands were handcuffed to a metal slot behind her, it had taken the entire time to get to the bottom of her foot. Maneuvering under constant watch had made it even more difficult than she'd originally hoped.

Cold and shaking, she pulled off her shoe. Yanking at the lump in her sock, working it until she could feel the little switch to turn the locater on. Then she relaxed. It

was done. If anyone was watching for her GPS they could find her now.

Wherever that might be.

"Come on, Levi." She desperately prayed her plan would work. *It should work. It has to work.*

Rolling her shoulders, she tried to work through the pain and stiffness. The windowless van grew darker and smaller with each beat of her heart. A horrible closed-in feeling took control. She couldn't move. The thundering in her ears faded to a thump-thump, thump-thump, thump-thump.

No longer in the van, she saw the white inside boards of the toy box her father had built. She could see her name— *EMALINE*—in thick crayon, a child's first writing attempt. Somehow the toys stayed on the floor, and her blanket and pillow were inside with her. They always were.

*I'm not really here. I'm not really here.* She could tell herself over and over again, but she couldn't force her eyes open to see anything else and the feeling trapped her in the past.

Real memory? Imagined because of what Levi had told her?

Rainbows. Lots of rainbows. Her mother smiled—just a blurred image of dark hair and happiness. She didn't want to leave the rainbows. Her mother laughed and said she'd bring them in her pocket. Grownups laughed with her saying it was fine.

Pop. Then another. The men fell. Her mother screamed. "Mama!" she heard a young, small voice—shrill and hysterical. Pinned. Held. Watching. Her mother screamed to shut her eyes. The door opened. She broke free, went to her mother. Heard her father yell, "Run!"

The crayon *EMALINE* was covered in dripping red. She'd been in the toy box, *after* she'd been in the kitchen. The lid was closed. Her cheeks were wet. She swiped her

tiny fingers at the wood over and over. She'd been in the kitchen. She'd run upstairs to her room.

A voice called to her. Coaxing her to come out. What were they saying? Why couldn't she understand?

The memory shattered and stopped. Her eyes quickly adjusted to the dark inside of the van again and she could hear voices. Real voices, not those from her childhood.

"Don't argue—If you'd killed her—wouldn't be in— situation."

Jo could hear words during the lull of the screaming music. A woman—just out of Jo's view—raised her voice. The man arguing with her was the one who had shot LuLu. She hadn't seen the driver's face or heard him speak. He stood with his back next to the van, in front of the cracked side door, continuing his silence.

"We—found Elaine's—"

Using her shoulder, Jo shoved at the headphones, moving one off her ear.

"Both. Do you understand?" the woman commanded.

"She was five," said the driver.

"That's no longer the case." The woman added a distinguishing snort of disgust. "Why did you need to see me before finishing this project?"

"The marshal demanded to meet with you. That wasn't in the plan. He says he has evidence to exchange."

"If the FBI had anything, they would have already contacted my office searching for me. You're an idiot and I don't know why I've continued to do business with you."

"My brother and I have your secrets stored in a safe place."

His attitude sent shivers down Jo's spine. The shooter had looked so evil, but now sounded even more so.

"Question her and the marshal and then make their bod-

ies disappear. We need to be extremely careful over the next few months. No contact."

"Right."

"I'm returning to the dinner and don't want to be disturbed again. Take care of this problem and earn your share. We've been successful for longer than that stupid girl's been alive and will continue to be once she's dead."

The sound of the woman's heels echoing through the empty space sent more shivers through her body than when LuLu had been shot. *Kill us and make us disappear.* How many people had died at this man's hands? Because of this woman?

"We go to the meet…No, we shouldn't risk disposing of the bodies in the same spot." He paused as if he was having a conversation with the driver still at the door of the van. "Maybe a trip to Louisiana, bodies don't resurface from those swamps. I've got your back. You can trust your big brother."

She had to get out of there. Her plan had been the most stupid plan on earth.

"Right, I knew you'd like that idea. We'll divide and conquer when we meet up with her boyfriend. I'm taking a leak, then we're moving out. Is the bat in front or back?"

She flexed and pointed her toes, fighting the effects from being motionless. Shaking would alert her captors and she didn't want them to know she was ready to escape. She also worked the headphone back onto her ear. There'd be aspirin for the headache when she escaped. It was better if they didn't know she'd overheard them. The evil-grinned man opened the side door wider and removed the baseball bat. His leer made her stomach turn and she looked past him to see a parking garage sign and pillar.

Jo thought she'd have a stronger emotional reaction to them. Hate the murderers clearly responsible for the deaths

of her parents. Be scared they planned to kill Levi. But she didn't panic. Didn't head to a dark, horrible memory.

Instead she went to those moments in the motor home bedroom, glad to remember anything good. And the time she'd had with Levi was wonderful, gave her strength. He'd find her. These men underestimated not only her determination, but everything about the man she loved.

The door was shut. Locked. In order to save her sanity she worked the headphones off her head. Despite her chill, enough moisture had accumulated on her lip to help her loosen the tape. She pulled and stretched her mouth, slowly working her way free to warn Levi before he found them.

Her plan had definitely put Levi in danger...but she couldn't stand the thought he'd be ambushed and beaten.

He'd come.

Levi would keep his promise.

Levi exited Interstate 30 and was caught at a light behind another car. He enlarged the map on his phone and verified that the location of the GPS was directly in front of him, about five miles north of where he was supposed to meet the kidnappers.

The Dallas Convention Center loomed against the backdrop of city lights with cars lining the street for a function. He spotted the words *Academy* and *Fine Arts* but headed straight on the frontage road until he came to a security booth.

"Excuse me." He waited on the older man sitting inside to step outside into the cold. "Have any trouble with extra vehicles hanging around or anything out of place tonight?"

"Just as borin' as always."

"What's going on back there?" He tilted his head toward the Academy.

"Political fundraiser. Lots of big wigs. Lots of extra security."

Levi flipped his marshal ID open for the man to look over. "Mind if I take a look around?"

"Go right ahead. Makes me no never mind." The disinterested guard stepped back into the booth and shut the door.

Levi drove the truck just inside the entrance and parked, dialing Lanning.

"About time you checked in."

"I assume you know I'm following the signal to the Convention Center?" Levi had already seen Lanning's supplies in the locked toolbox. He used the key and pulled out an FBI issued vest.

"We're ten minutes out. Wait for backup."

"Can't. They'll pull out for the exchange soon. No police. I need the edge." He finished the pulls.

"Cooper—"

"No cops, Lanning. You know they'll kill her."

No more wasted time on conversation. Using his phone to guide him closer to the GPS gadget, he ran through the parking garage keeping his weapon drawn. There was no way to tell what level the GPS was on, he could only hope the people holding her captive had stuck to the fastest exit. The lowest floor.

"You stupid idiot. Cooper's at the exit. Get her out of the van."

Jolene prepared for the hurt the next moves were going to cost her. She'd twisted low enough on the floor of the van to pull her knees to her chest. Her shoulders throbbed, but if she could catch one of them off guard…

The door opened. Thank God LuLu's murderer was looking away from Jo toward the man talking to him. He

reached inside and she kicked him full force in the face, screaming, "It's a trap!"

The man fell backward. She heard the metal bat hit the concrete floor. The men scrambled.

With her heart racing, wondering if they'd think a bullet to *her* head was their fastest escape route, she tugged again and again at the cuffs. There was no way to pull free. She was a sitting duck, but hopefully Levi had been warned. The men ran from the van—maybe for cover she couldn't see.

Gunfire.

Lots of gunfire.

Then nothing.

What had happened? She was afraid to call out and remind her captors she was there.

"Jo?" Levi's voice was the sweetest sound to her pounding ears.

"I'm in here."

"You okay?" His voice sounded closer.

"Handcuffed, but okay."

The van shook a bit as he opened the front door. "No ignition keys, but these look like they're to cuffs."

Then his anxious face appeared at the side door. One last look behind him and he was inside the van. Jo had already turned—facing away—so he'd have faster access to her wrists. "I knocked one of those guys unconscious. Not sure where the other one is. Can you walk?"

"Just get me out of this van." She shook her hands and legs, waking them up completely. Fighting the sensation of pinpricks was much preferred to remaining a prisoner.

"Yeah, well that may be more of a problem than I originally thought." Levi pointed to one of her kidnappers shaking LuLu's murderer awake and disappearing behind

a pillar. Her rescuer changed the clip in his gun and re-loaded the one he'd removed.

"The stairs are behind us and to the left." He pointed in the direction so she'd know exactly where he meant. "I'll lay down cover and you run."

"But—"

"No buts, Jo. This is me taking over."

"Yes, sir. Absolutely." She meant it. He was in charge. She pulled the tracker out of her sock, shoved it in her jeans pockets and pulled her shoe back on. "Where to after that? I don't know where I'm at."

"Up. We'll deal with the rest once we make it across the garage." Levi cracked open the rear door.

They were both poised, prepared to leap after he threw it open. Levi's gun was up.

"You ready?" he asked. "Wait. Put this on."

Before she could argue or tell him it was more important for him not to get shot, he had the FBI bulletproof vest over her head and was pulling the straps tight.

"I knew you'd find me."

"For the record I'm furious, but if we didn't need to escape yet another *death trap*—as you call them, I'd be kissing you 'til tomorrow."

She was speechless. Plain and simple, she hadn't expected those words. By the astonished look rippling across his face, maybe he hadn't expected to say them. He quickly turned, took a look out the door, pushed it open and began shooting.

Jo ran.

# Chapter Nineteen

Their goal was a good hundred feet away. Then what? Run until Lanning and his team found them? That was the plan?

Levi stood behind the van door and fired a couple of shots in the direction Jo's kidnappers had been. She ran and he covered her until she was through the door. Another shot. Not his. And he felt the searing pain in his calf.

He'd been looking out for Jo's safety instead of tracking where the shooters were. Returning fire, he ran while he still could. If he allowed the pain to take over, Jo would be dead.

*You stop, she's dead.* The mantra replayed through his head as the pain splintered through each step. *You stop, she's dead.*

"Not," he grunted, forcing the words, "happening."

Jo pushed the door open as he approached. She'd pulled the vest off and was yanking her shirt over her head.

"What are you—"

She knelt and tied the shirtsleeves around his leg as a bandage. He checked his cell.

"That's the best I can do. Now what?"

"Still no signal so we keep moving until the FBI swoops in for the save." He raised his eyes up at the staircase. No way to block the door and a heck of a lot of stairs to climb. "We go up. Put the vest back on."

She swung the vest on as they moved. The pain in his leg reminded him with every step what would happen to Jo if he failed. They got into a rhythm. He followed—protecting her from behind—until they reached a new level. She waited, he verified no one was there, they climbed another flight.

Three more flights and they found the main lobby level. Then Levi heard footsteps slapping against the concrete beneath them. He verified their path was clear and turned to her. "Nearest door and we're outside, flagging down a car."

"Got it. You okay?"

"I got a couple of sprints left in me."

Jo grabbed his hand and turned in the direction the arrows had pointed to the lobby.

"She was here, Levi," she whispered. "My mother's client. The woman responsible for all this destruction. She's the reason they brought me here after they murdered LuLu."

"Did you get her name?"

She shook her head and punched open the door to the main corridor.

"We'll go over everything. First we have to get out of this building."

They discovered multiple doors leading toward a park. All locked. Main lobby on their right, street on their left. They kept running until they found an emergency exit. Just as they heard the alarm sound, the slam of the stairwell door against the wall echoed through the empty hall.

The man following them made excellent time catching up. The bullet wound had slowed Levi down more than he cared to admit. The street and the Omni Hotel were within sight. Only one guy chased them on foot, but both had shot at him. The second man was in the van. The vulture

was waiting for the kill. There had been plenty of time for him to drive from the garage and be in place to cut them off at the street.

"We need to find cover."

The man on foot still had to run the length of the building to get to the open door.

"But I thought—"

"The van's sure to be waiting to cut us down as we cross the street. Move it, Jo."

They headed for the shadows, just out of the spotlight circling a larger-than-life statue of a cowboy wrangling longhorns. They hid in the darkness and tall grass. It wouldn't last long, the shadows barely large enough for them both and not nearly dark enough to disguise them from someone walking past.

"Where are the cops? Or your friendly FBI? Didn't they want to tag along for the fun?" she asked, untying the sleeves of her shirt, rolling it and making a bandage of sorts under his pants leg. "This looks bad."

"Bad and I wouldn't be able to walk. I'm fine. You're in a chipper mood. You forgetting that you almost died back there?"

"I remember. But once you arrived, I didn't think about dying. By the way, you're getting slow," she whispered with a grin and yanked harder on the sleeves.

The jolt of agony blasted through his entire body.

A bullet pinged off a bronze longhorn. He turned back and discharged his weapon to keep the shooter pinned behind an oak tree.

"Jo." He grabbed her shoulder with his free hand, forcing her to look at him. "You're going to run up that hill, get across the street and call Lanning. He should be close."

"Does Lanning have the GPS info?"

"Yeah."

He handed her his cell, whispering as firmly as he could without being overheard. "Just like in the garage. You lead the way. I'll be close behind."

She understood and nodded her head.

"I'll lay down cover and you run." One step backward and his hand dropped. He took a couple of shots and she took off. She didn't let the gunfire slow her down.

Another shot hit a tree trunk just behind him, coming a little too close. He laid down cover fire and got to his feet to follow.

"Watch out for the horn," Jo cautioned.

He faced forward just in time to miss taking a two-foot longhorn across his neck. She waited long enough to see him miss it, then darted between the statues and the rock ledge up the path.

He had less and less feeling in his foot and it was harder to move. They'd made it across the cattle drive sculpture and into a cemetery at the top of the slope. A frickin' cemetery in front of him and an empty convention center to his right, closed businesses across to his left, and the driver of the van on the road behind him.

"Which way?" she asked. "Can you make it to the road?"

"No good, we don't know where the driver is."

"Then we go through the cemetery. We keep moving until George finds us. That's what you said, right?"

He doubted it. But he waved her onward. He had no intention of following the entire distance. He couldn't. The footsteps slogging up the hill were closer. The guy chasing was certain to see them with the multicolored neon lights from the Omni illuminating the place like the Vegas strip.

She darted to the next tombstone, then a tree, her silhouette as plain as if a spotlight shone upon her path.

It was imperative to stop the guy following them before

he caught up with Jo. He searched the darkness. Waited for movement. Had the perp skirted the outside of the cemetery? Had he just sent Jo into an ambush?

*Hide on the back side of the building and call Lanning,* he instructed even knowing she couldn't hear him.

To his right. Next tree. Ten or twelve feet. *There's the bastard.*

No time for stealth. Levi stepped into the open. "That's far enough."

Taken by surprise, the man turned and fired. Levi dove and hit the damp leaves. Rolled. The man got closer. Levi fired twice. He didn't miss.

The man dropped to the ground covering a gravestone with his still body.

"Levi?"

Jo ran to him, tree branch in hand, ready to help as much as she could. He hadn't moved since LuLu's murderer had fallen. She hated to wish anyone dead, but this man had shot her old babysitter without a moment's hesitation.

She could hear sirens approaching. Heard a train whistle in the distance. And oddly, the lights shining through the trees and rippling across the tall hotel were beautiful blues, pinks and purples.

She dropped the stick.

Levi blew a long, forceful breath through his lips as he got to his feet. He limped to the body, kneeling on his good leg to feel for a pulse. Then he shook his head, confirming death. "Was this *Rainbow Man*?"

"I don't know, but he's the one that shot LuLu."

"What about the other guy?"

From the corner of her eye, something flew from behind a tall tombstone.

"Watch out!"

A knife.

She ducked and knocked Levi off balance and they were both on the ground. A guttural wrenching cry split the air, as the man leapt for his long blade.

"Get out of here, Jo! Get help."

Easier said than done. The crazed man was still rolling across her legs, pinning her to the ground. Levi had the man by his hands, stopping him from reaching the weapon. In return, the driver straddled Levi, pinning him next to his dead partner.

Jo pulled the phone, wasting precious seconds finding Lanning's number. "We're in a cemetery. Levi needs help."

"We're almost there." Lanning's voice faded as she tossed the phone behind her, hoping they'd be found quickly.

She tripped over a branch. It was the only weapon she could find. She swung at the man, heard a grunt. The man pounded Levi's kidneys. The men struggled for dominance, constantly changing positions. But if she found the gun, she could save Levi.

As bright as she'd thought the neon lit night had been, it barely illuminated the ground. She dropped to her knees, feeling for the cold metal of the weapon. She let her eyes adjust to the darkness again. There it was. She got her hands around the handle and a cold hand pried at her fingers.

"Levi!"

The man grunted, pushing her underneath him, sitting across her hips, jerking her arm under his knee to hold it in place. Her hand gripped the gun but was pinned to the ground and quickly going numb. She had to break free. Had to help Levi! She kicked her legs. Shoved with her body.

The man backhanded her. Her face was on fire from the sting of the slap. Her eyes watered and his face contorted

into a menagerie of evil creatures. Images that had haunted her far too long. She couldn't beat him with strength and relaxed, letting the gun go.

The same lecherous smile his brother had used spread across his face. His hand slipped around her throat, squeezing just enough to limit her air, but keep her conscious. Both hands tightened around her throat, strangling her with his icy fingers. Her heart was pounding loudly in her ears, hard against her ribs, short bursts of air, then nothing. And then her lungs worked again.

Levi had knocked the man away from her. Thank God he was still alive. She was still alive. But they wouldn't be for long if she didn't find the gun. She ignored how the man was hurting Levi and concentrated on one thing— the gun.

She grabbed the gun. She pointed. Slowly. Carefully. *You can't take anything else from me!*

The shattering blast in his side knocked the attacker off Levi.

"They're over here!"

Levi took the gun from her, pointing at the horrible creature, who crawled to the dead man at their feet and signed, trying to communicate. She couldn't watch.

"He's mute," she whispered with a raspy, hurt sound.

"Someone stop the bleeding and try to record what he's saying." George directed agents and police officers. "How far out is the bus?"

"This one's dead, sir."

People were suddenly everywhere.

"Get Jolene a blanket."

She thought George gave that direction, too, but the world got smaller and became just her and Levi. "Are you okay?" she asked.

"Ready to take that vest off? Sorry I can't give you back

your shirt." Levi pulled his over his head and wrapped it around her.

The warmth and safety of his arms made everything tolerable. An officer handed Levi a blanket, which he used around them both. She was thankful, because his strength helped her hold everything together.

He brought her closer to his chest. "I'm not letting you out of my sight."

"You've been shot. You need a hospital." She tried to back away, but he squeezed her tighter. The warmth of his chest spread across her skin.

"I'm serious, Jo. Right next to me, every step of the way."

"Why would I want to leave?"

THE ENTIRE AREA looked like the end of a movie. Emergency lights flashed on the city street next to tape cordoning off the crime scene. Even down to Jo holding hands with the handsome bare-chested hero who had given her his shirt after getting shot while saving her. At this point in the movie, the hero and heroine would kiss, say I love you and go off to live happily ever after.

Too bad this was reality and not the movies and not the time to tell Levi she loved him. Surrounded by strangers, watching them take away the men who had tried to kill them. At least he wasn't seriously injured. He still needed to go to the hospital, but continued to keep the EMTs waiting.

Details of "the incident" were recounted to first the FBI and then the police. She'd answered all their questions even after Levi had insisted she was too tired and should sit in a patrol car.

It really did feel like the end of something. An era in her life was finished and the opportunities she hadn't al-

lowed herself to consider before were now possible. What did she want?

*Levi.*

Another officer tried to escort her to the sidelines. She'd accepted the blanket around her shoulders so she could warm up and a bottle of water to hydrate, but she stayed by Levi's side. The EMTs bandaged his leg, stuck a needle in his arm and kept insisting they needed to get him to the hospital. He finally conceded to leave after a whispered conversation with George.

"Would I be an ass if I tell you never to put yourself in danger like that again?" Levi had at least waited until they were semi-alone. He took her hand, more gently than she anticipated and rested them both on his abdomen. His eyes shut, looking like the gunshot had finally caught up with him.

"I think this discussion should wait. You're exhausted."

"I'd like to know why you risked your life and didn't trust me." He held her hand tightly, keeping it secure next to his cool skin.

"It was my risk to take. My decision."

"You really don't think that decision had anything to do with me?"

"Can we talk about this tomorrow?"

"I'd like to know, Jo. If you almost killing yourself didn't involve me after the time we've spent together this past week and the promise I made to your father, then what do we have?"

Jo could feel the eyes of strangers on her. EMTs and a couple of policemen standing nearby weren't trying to be polite and give them privacy. Very embarrassed, she tried to pull her hand free, but Levi held tight, a determined look on his face.

Thankfully, the EMTs interrupted. She stepped back as

they lifted the gurney. Levi's lips were in a thin line—was it disappointment or pain? Maybe a little of both.

"Sorry, sir," the EMT shifting his IV fluid said. "No ride-alongs."

"She can't be left here alone. Can't you say she needs to be checked out or something?"

"Are you okay, miss?"

"Fine. He's delusional and forgetting I'm not ten."

"We've got to move out, Marshal." The second EMT climbed in the back with him while the first stood ready to shut the door.

"Jo, promise me you'll stick close to Lanning. Promise."

"Fine. I'll stick close to George and have him bring me to the hospital."

"I need you to walk her back to Agent Lanning," he said to the technician climbing into the van with him.

"Sorry, man. We've got to take off. There's lots of cops around. She's safe."

"Come on, make sure she gets back." She heard him say behind the closed doors, continuing to worry about her.

"I'll be fine, Levi!" she shouted to the closed door, feeling extremely tired. Maybe she'd rest in that patrol car after all. She'd tell her protector how sorry she was at the hospital. She hadn't meant to hurt him. She'd show him how much he meant in her life.

In spite of the fatigue she felt a new emotion—hope. She hadn't given herself permission to believe everything would be okay. Was she ready for her normal life to resume? Which life? Georgia or Colorado? Too many questions for right that minute.

Without the emergency lights flashing, the night seemed to creep in on her again. The full force of what had happened in the past week—especially today—hit her be-

tween her shoulders. She was suddenly very tired. Ready for sleep tired.

A normal reaction to no longer running and avoiding danger. Adrenaline or endorphins did that to people. Right? Maybe she had hit her head. Her vision wasn't as clear and she felt sort of woozy. The water bottle dropped from her fingers, bouncing along the sidewalk. She wanted to pick it up. She tried. Following its path as the wind continued to blow it became more difficult with every step.

"Let me get that for you, dear."

The woman in front of her was familiar. Why did she care? She needed to sit down. Standing was too tiring.

"Come along, dear. I'll help."

The woman wrapped her arm around Jo's waist and led her away from the flashing lights, around the corner of the convention center, away from…it was important. She had to remember. Away from…

"My promise. I know your voice." The van. The woman yelling outside the van.

"Brava, Emaline. Your mother and father would be so proud of you." The older woman put her in the passenger seat, put the seat belt into place and took something from the glove compartment. Her wrists were slapped together and tied. Burning, hurting.

"I came to finish our—shall we say—chapter."

"Who? I shouldn't be here." She tried to unbuckle, but her hands were so heavy. "Drugs?"

"That's right. Sleepy time now."

*Don't be mad, Levi. I tried to keep my promise.*

# *Chapter Twenty*

"What do you mean she's not with you?"

"I thought she was here with you." Lanning didn't act concerned. He sat in a chair looking satisfied. "She probably took a cab back to the motor home. I've already sent locals there. Give it a minute."

"It's been a couple of hours and she promised to stay with you." Panic again. He thought he was past this utter terror regarding her safety. Jo was supposed to be secured by the FBI.

"You need to accept that your girlfriend makes her own decisions."

"I shouldn't have left her."

"You were shot."

"Scratched."

"I don't know why I'm trying to make you feel better. You're the one that owes me eternal gratitude." Lanning answered his phone on the second buzz. A few seconds in and he faced the door, lowering his voice.

It didn't take a great investigator to figure out the news wasn't good. Levi rang for the nurse and swung his legs from under the blanket.

"Can I help you?" a voice said through the speaker.

"I need this IV out now."

"Mr. Cooper, the doctor wants to keep you overnight—"

"Not happening."

"If you can't walk, you aren't leaving," Lanning said.

"I'm leaving."

"Then let's get you out of here." Lanning swung the door open and waved his arm at the nurse station. "We're leaving. Get him some clothes."

Things happened at a swift pace when an FBI Agent made demands. Levi opened his mouth to ask about the phone call and Lanning shook his head.

"No one saw her after I left?" Levi asked as soon as they were in Lanning's truck. "You shrugged off that she'd heard a woman in the garage who seemed to be in charge."

"Blame me. Cuss me. Whatever. But do it later. Work with me. We'll be at headquarters in a few minutes. They've assembled security footage, cameras from area buildings, along with footage we gathered from the event at the Arts Academy." He raised an eyebrow. "Yeah, I took her seriously. We were already cross-referencing to see if someone had anything to do with Miller or Phillips and came up with two possibles."

"Glad you're on top of it." That was as close to an apology as Lanning would get from him. "What about the GPS signal? She may still be transmitting."

"Barlow, Atkins still has the transmitter. Get its location.

Levi removed his phone from the bagged items, cursed himself while it powered up, and keyed open the tracking site. "Turn around. She's at the Frasiers' old house."

"This is Special Agent Lanning and I need units dispatched to…"

"Hang on just one more time, Jo."

JO HAD NEVER had a serious hangover in her life, but if she had to imagine how one would feel…this was it. Groggy,

she stayed on the passenger seat with no desire to move. Each time she did, pain shot through her skull in every direction.

The door opened and she rolled her head to look straight into a gun barrel.

"Wake up and walk. It's time for us to…chat."

Jo sat forward with a little less discomfort than the first time she'd tried. The effects were wearing off, but she was still wobbly when she stood. Her wrists, on the other hand, were quite raw from the rope twisted on top of the cuts left from the handcuffs. They were inside a home garage with the outside door shut.

"Who are you?"

"You don't remember me, dear? That would have been good to know several months ago. *Before* I began looking for you and your father."

"What do you want?"

"Why, the carving, of course." She pointed the pistol toward the door leading inside the house.

"Your men handed it to you at the van." This was her house. The surroundings were familiar even though she didn't recognize anything specific. Stepping inside, she'd be near the kitchen. "I can't go in there."

"Let me make things a little clearer for you." The woman took a step closer and yanked Jo's head back by the roots of her hair. "You will go in and have a seat at the kitchen table. You will tell me where you left the carving. I have no use for incompetents."

Jo twisted her head free from the woman's grasp. She hurt more from the drug aftereffects and the loss of control to her runaway life. She faced the older woman, determined to get free and put an end to the madness.

"I will shoot you," the woman took a step back, bracing herself against the car.

There wasn't a way to knock the gun free. There was nowhere to run except through the house. She could feel the GPS locator still in the bottom of her jeans pocket and hoped the FBI knew she was missing. The door was unlocked and she slowly moved inside, unsure of what might be waiting.

Each time she'd faced a dark memory from this place, she'd shut down and gone on auto-pilot. Time to confront her demons. Her parents' murderers were dead or in jail. She could do this. She could conquer her fear of the unknown and her life would be different.

Entering the kitchen, she was surprised it was so full of light. She immediately had a sense of fear, just like before with Levi. This time he wasn't here to guide her through a blackout.

*There's no reason to try to remember. You have answers. You found the murderer. Concentrate on the here and now...not the past.* The gun stuck in her back kept the present very close.

"Sit in the chair. I'm not in the mood to be toyed with girl. We both know there's a second dog. I want to know what you've done with it."

"Who are you?" Jo asked. "Why did you kill my parents?"

"Mrs. Albert Price-Reed, but Mrs. Price will do. Your parents were intent on destroying me."

Jo sat in a chair. Before she could focus her gaze, Mrs. Price whacked her across the temple with the butt of the gun.

"A reminder that I'm asking the questions and expect answers."

It took Jo a second to get her head to stop spinning. "We both know you're going to kill me..." *Come on, Levi, you*

*do the hero thing and make sure to save me. The sooner,
the better.*

"I've been at this in real life for over thirty years." Mrs.
Price took a step back and laughed. "I'd like to fill you in,
but I just don't have time."

Jo looked closer at the woman. She wore heavy, thick
makeup and although her silver hair was thinning it was
puffed up on top of her head. With the lights behind her it
appeared almost…blue.

"You're…you're the *Rainbow Man*. Those men didn't
kill my mother, it was you!"

"Are you still obsessing over rainbows like a child?"

"Why didn't you kill me back then?"

Price's lip turned up in a sneer. "An off day, I'm afraid.
I didn't verify that you or your father were actually dead.
I left it to Tweetle Dumb and Tweetle Dumber. A mistake
that's been hanging over my head for twenty years. We
found one statue but not the other."

"There's nothing inside. The large one doesn't have a
secret compartment."

"How little you know. Where is it?" Price demanded.

"I imagine the FBI has it by now."

"Then you're of no use to me." She turned her back
on Jo and crossed to the corner table, picking up a long-
bladed knife.

Jo should have lied, told the old woman that she could
take her to the carving. The answers to questions that had
haunted her entire life were behind those thin lips.

"You killed my parents for family carvings?"

"Carvings? No. Your mother planned to expose me."
She set the gun down on the counter, selecting a knife,
waving it next to her ear. "My father had been doing business with Elaine for years. When he…*died,* I took over
with improvements. Everything was going fine until the

digital era hit. Your mother hired someone to create a database and when the information came together, she discovered I had dummy corporations, et cetera, et cetera."

"It doesn't sound like a reason she'd need witness protection."

"You do like to talk, don't you?" She pulled knives from the wooden block, examining each tip and edge. "She discovered how we'd duped the government and then covered up the loose ends."

"You mean by killing more people?"

*Distract her. Keep her talking until Levi arrived.* Or she could free herself. Honestly, the drug she'd been given had her skeptical of standing for long. All she had to do was wake up the next door neighbors. Surely she could outrun this blue-haired, heartless killer to the next house. Keep her talking and distracted.

"What do my father's carvings have to do with any of this?"

"Robert was very good with his hands." She laughed, deep, almost hysterical. When she finished she dabbed at the corner of her heavily lidded eyes. "Your mother treasured those two carvings above everything else. One here, one at her office. When they were missing after your family's deaths, I suspected that's where she'd hidden the evidence. Then we found one in that birdhouse. But only one and nothing was inside. So where is it?"

"Why kill my father? Or me? We didn't know any of this."

"I didn't know how to ask before recently." She flipped the knife over and over, staring at the blade while the light reflected onto the wall. "You aren't expecting a last-minute rescue, are you? Isn't your boyfriend in the hospital?"

The psycho was right. She'd been hoping and praying that Levi would follow the tracker. Without him, no one

knows to look for her. That settled her inner debate. Even woozy, she should be able to defeat this frail sicko.

"You won't get away with killing me. You can't walk into a room, commit murder and not leave evidence." If she could just get the witch frassled, she could get out the garage door. "It's the age of technology. Even if you wore gloves, your DNA is dropping clues everywhere you walk. They're already on my clothes. They'll find a connection and you'll spend your last days on death row. Texas does have the death penalty, right?"

"Impressive and exactly the reason I plan to destroy everything. It's time I turned a profit on this property." The woman captured the look of a calm, deadly killer. Her mother's murder hadn't been rage or an accident. This woman enjoyed killing.

There wouldn't be any mercy or change of heart from this geriatric psychopath. Jo would be murdered if she didn't find a way out of the house. She jerked at the rope tying her hands.

The click-clack of heels coming toward her across the bare floor drew her focus on escape. She braced one leg on the floor and got ready to kick. It had worked in the van to buy her time. Hopefully it would again. The woman approached, knife ready to slice. Jo lashed out. The woman screamed, and bent in half before falling to her knees.

Jo jumped up and kicked again, running toward the counter where Price had laid the gun. It wasn't there. She'd moved it. Where? Was the loud scream from her or the crazed woman running at her across the kitchen? Jo grabbed something off the counter, threw it using both hands. Then some type of figurine. And then a small dish while backing out of the room, holding off the advancing knife.

Then she recognized the steel barrel in her grasp. She

fumbled, twirling it to fit in her grip. She saw the blade out of the corner of her eye, headed toward her shoulder. She swung her arms that direction, heard the metal hit the tile floor. Price followed the knife.

"Stay there," she yelled. "I will shoot you!"

"You can't do it," Price said from the floor.

"It's hard *not* to pull the trigger. You murdered my parents."

The woman reached again for the kitchen knife she'd planned to cut Jo's throat with. Jo wasn't threatened, but she tilted the gun to the ceiling and squeezed off three rounds.

Price's silvery, elderly skin froze in an astonished look of surprise. Jo aimed the gun once again at the murderer.

"As much as I hate you, I'm going to let the neighbors call the cops. I'm going to answer all their questions. I'm going to testify. I'll go back into witness protection if that's what it takes to put you in prison for the rest of your miserable life. Sit tight or I'll blow a hole in your arm, but I won't kill you. I want you to rot."

Jo must have sounded a lot more competent than she felt. Or maybe Price was just waiting for her to keel over from the exertion. Minutes passed without Price moving a muscle or uttering a sound.

"Plano PD. Drop the weapon."

"This woman drugged and kidnapped me," Jo said. "George Lanning at the FBI will—"

"I'm Judge Albert Price's wife. Arrest that woman for assault."

Sirens. Someone cut her hands loose. She sat.

Jo remained silent while Price jabbered about her abduction from a fundraising dinner. Everything was hazy. Jo drifted back to rainbows twirling around the kitchen. A dark-haired woman, laughing and smiling at her. A

younger, happier dad swooping her into his arms and dancing with them both.

*That* was the memory she'd keep and remember for the future. Price had tried to steal her family and failed.

"You okay, Jo?" The voice she so desperately wanted to hear spoke close to her ear. Her hero, no matter how much he hated movie comparisons.

The FBI had arrived along with a perfectly healthy Levi. She'd done it. Her parents could rest. So could she. Levi took her into his arms and got her outside. It might have been the impact of whatever drug was still in her system, the blow to her head or just the fact no one was trying to kill her any longer. But she was suddenly cold and shivering.

"Hang on, Jo. We'll leave as soon as the EMTs get you checked out."

There were questions and shouts. Raised voices. Blurs around her that she knew were law enforcement. She kept her face in Levi's chest, unable to watch.

"How's she doing?" someone asked, maybe George.

"She's in shock. Where are the EMTs?"

She wanted to reassure Levi she was okay. She was exhausted and just wanted to get out of there.

"Stay with me, Jo. Lanning, I need your keys. We aren't waiting." He lifted her into his arms.

Tight and secure she was able to look long enough into those dark eyes and see none of the chaos around her. "Don't let go."

His lips lingered on her forehead for just a moment, then he smiled crookedly. "I won't, Jo. Not ever."

## Chapter Twenty-One

"I thought I'd lost you," Levi whispered into Jo's hair and leaving another feather-light kiss.

The doctors were finished. Her wrists had been cleaned and bandaged. Bruises on her temple and jaw were darkening. Levi sat in the hospital bed with her sleeping cradled in his arms. He could lift her into the second patient bed, but she seemed comfortable enough curled to his side, legs stretched across him, cheek resting on his chest. It was more for his benefit than her security, and it had helped her fall asleep.

One of Lanning's agents was at their room door. He could drift off, catch a nap, knowing she was safe. His witness—that wasn't a witness—was finally under his protection.

"Good morning."

"Lanning." Levi opened his eyes. He must have really slept. Sunshine poured through the window. He squinted at the clock. "Ten o'clock?"

Jo snuggled a bit more adding a little groan of protest when he shifted his arm.

"Your phone's off. Turn it on. Boss lady called to say she wants you on the first plane back to Denver. You've been reinstated." Lanning made himself comfortable in the corner chair. "I think she wants to be awake for this."

"I'm awake. I was hoping you'd feel guilty and maybe leave." She sat next to him on the bed.

Levi moved his arm and meshed his fingers through hers to keep her next to him. That second bed could stay empty. She accepted his unspoken direction and tucked the blanket closer around her legs.

"Docs said you can both leave the hospital soon. Question is...where do you go?" Lanning held up his hand. "Hold on. Before you go jumping down my throat, Cooper, I've arranged protective custody for your girl until the trial or we determine that no one else wants her out of the picture."

"Is that really necessary? I don't even know why Price-Reed wanted my family dead or what it was about."

"That I do know. Carol Price-Reed was the wife of a Dallas County judge and daughter of a Texas real estate giant who was greedier than either of the men in her life." Lanning tapped the thick file on his lap. "They're having a field day discovering all the crooked business dealings she's been associated with over the past thirty or forty years. So many illegal companies that they're splitting up jurisdiction. The names inside the dog were the missing connection."

"Dad left a clue? Why didn't you tell me?" She faced Levi, accusing him of withholding information.

"Wait a minute. You sort of took off on your own before I found it and I've been a little busy rescuing you."

The bed that had barely been big enough to hold them suddenly had a lot more room as Jo pulled away to the edge.

Lanning cleared his throat and they both turned back to him. "The names provided by your father, Miller and Phillips, appear to be as innocent as your mother. Connecting the banker, the appraiser and the title work your

mother sometimes did, unraveled all the carefully twisted lies and layers of dummy corporations."

"Why didn't anyone make the connection earlier and what stirred the pot for another investigation last year? Is Jo still at risk?"

"Did the mute survive? And is Price-Reed talking yet?" Jo asked at the same time.

"I knew you'd have questions." Lanning smiled at Jo. "They both lawyered up as soon as the cuffs were on. The mute and his brother were ID'd from their prints and a long list of wrongs as Sonny and Tommy Smith. Seems Judge Price kept them out of prison more than once, probably had something to do with the investigation twenty years ago. Sonny's lawyer says he has evidence to put Price-Reed away for the rest of her days. They're talking to the DoJ."

"Then why do I need to go into hiding?" Jo's body stiffened, her hands going to the edge of the blanket, ready to pull it back and stand.

Levi shifted, holding her hand tighter, shaking his head to discourage her leaving his side. "After what you've been through, I'd think you'd welcome it." He had to convince her to take the protection. No matter how much he wanted her next to him, this was the only way to assure her safety. She had to understand.

"I think I've proven that I can take care of myself."

"But you don't need to worry about proving yourself," Levi stressed. Jo's mouth formed a thin line. He was close enough to hear her jaw pop as the result of gnashing her molars. This is what he did. He protected people. He could protect her with the proper resources.

"Don't mind me, the sleepless FBI agent that saved both your hides. I'd leave, but I need to arrange what happens next."

Jo showed him the back of her shoulder, essentially ig-

noring him and his experience. "Sorry, George, but do you really think I'm in any danger?"

"I can't force you to—"

"Yes, you can." Levi leaned forward, cupping her chin to guide it to face him before he pleaded, "Take it."

Jo turned a frosty gaze to him. Something he hadn't seen since the funeral. She stood with jerky movements, making certain her elbow caught him a couple of times below the ribs. She secured the blanket around her shoulders and marched barefoot to the now standing Lanning. He ignored her extended hand and pulled her close for a Texas hug, smirking over her shoulder and extending the gesture a tad longer than necessary. Levi was about to jump out of the bed when Jo broke off the embrace.

"George, I appreciate your arrangements. But if that's the only option, then we're done. I'll, of course, make myself available for whatever the FBI needs."

Levi looked at George then at her. Gaping at them was probably a better description. He couldn't believe what was happening. "That's it? You're just going to let her walk away?"

"I can't force her into protective custody. You, of all people, know that." If Lanning's cocky smile meant anything, it was that he'd be glad to take up where Levi had left off.

"Go back to your life, Levi," Jo said. "You have your job back. I need some time."

"Jo. You can't turn this down. We've been trying to get you protection for a long time." Telling her what to do had never worked. Would never work. He silently cursed himself for not phrasing the words as a suggestion. "It's what your dad wanted."

The fierce need inside his chest hung on the edge of a precipice. Levi waited for her to agree. A look of embar-

rassment would confirm her consent. A look of encouragement would keep them talking, trying to convince each other of their side. And then, the look he'd dreaded, the one that confirmed she was leaving, sent his heart plunging to die a slow death.

"I know, Levi." She paused on her way out the door, trying to hide the tears pooling in her beautiful eyes. "I just…can't."

Everything about him that was a man missed her immediately. His arms missed the way she fit within their circle. The beat of his heart missed the echo of hers beneath her breasts. She'd been willing to sacrifice everything to get to this moment. The last thing between them would not be her walking away.

The days had been very long and lonely without him—not to mention the nights. She was trying to accept that the romantic part of their relationship was over. Harder still to accept their friendship was over.

Jolene stretched, enjoying the lumpy mattress. Lumpy was so much better than being hidden in a hotel for the past two nights while she gave her statements to the FBI. Car lights momentarily brightened her small bedroom, reminding her to get darkening curtains once she got on the road.

"To where?"

At this point she didn't care. Anywhere except Dallas. Any direction that didn't require turns until she got used to driving this huge monster. Get on a highway out of town and just keep going. She could do it. She could learn. And if she couldn't, she'd stop and take lessons. But she needed to get lost for a while, just turn whichever way wasn't blocked with red tape and a handsome U.S. Marshal.

She closed her eyes, attempting to fall asleep for the

countless time, excited for her big start in the morning. Her heart beat so fast she thought the motor home was moving.

"Wait." She threw her legs over the side and fell back when the wheels bounced over a speed bump. She charged through the door, prepared to pick up a frying pan if the driver wasn't the familiar head she expected in the driver's seat.

"Levi?"

"Did I wake you? You told Lanning you wanted to get an early start."

"Not at two in the morning. Pull over." The motor home was shifted into Park and he twisted in his seat to give her a sexy onceover look that had her squirming on the laminate floor. "I told George I didn't want to see you. Didn't he tell you?"

"I listened."

"You aren't supposed to be here. I wrote you a letter. I explained that I wanted to travel and you're going back to your job." Did she really want to leave him?

"I read it."

"It's better if I'm on my own for a while, to think." *To get over you.*

"Not happening." He shook his head and stood, shrinking the space between them. She wanted to run into his arms. She always did.

He stood straighter, appearing taller but somewhat less confident than he had a couple of days ago when she'd marched out of the hospital.

"Maybe I should take us back." He got behind the wheel and returned to their spot in the park. He stayed put in the driver's seat. "There were a couple of questions we saved for later."

"And this is later?" The need to take him to their bedroom was overwhelming, but he was right. There were

things they needed to settle, things she needed to know about what made Levi who he was.

"You asked me why I went along with your dad and lied to you all these years. First off, Joseph asked and I respected that, but I also gave him my word. About the same time, he sort of gave me the same talk my own dad did before he died."

"How old were you when you lost your dad?"

"Ten. My mom left Amarillo by the time I was two. High school sweethearts who made a mistake." He looked at ease, like he'd come to terms with his mother's decision a long time ago. "Both of our fathers spoke about how important it was to keep my word. That ultimately it was the only thing I had."

"You lived with the aunt you mentioned?"

"Yeah. We'd been living with my aunt and uncle most of my life already. I've always made it a point to keep my promises, Jo."

"You've more than kept your promise to my dad."

"That's not the promise I'm talking about." He paused a long time. "I promised not to let you go."

There was a look about Levi she hadn't really seen before. Something akin to petrified. He was afraid. He was really worried.

"That was when you rescued me. Levi, I didn't mean forever."

"But I did."

He swooped in and spun her around the small kitchen, kissing her mouth, making her want more. "So do I."

# *Epilogue*

"You're certain you're ready?" Levi asked Jo, slipping on his coat once they'd finalized everything with the Vegas wedding coordinator.

"Levi, you know everything there is to know about me. We've lived and traveled in a motor home from one side of the country to the other over the past six weeks." She put her hands on her hips like the spunky partner he'd had on the train just a short time ago. "I think you'd know by now when I've made up my mind."

Yeah, he knew. She'd taken a turn at the wheel of the motor home and headed them to Amarillo to pick up his aunt Catherine. She was the one who'd made hotel arrangements in Vegas and researched wedding chapels. Even arranged for him to have a best man.

"We don't have to do this now, today. We could wait." Levi took her hands, searching her eyes.

Calm. Hope. Excitement. Love. He could see the emotions waiting to be shared with him.

"Sounds like you're the one trying to back out," she teased.

"Not happening."

He pulled her into his arms to prove how much he wanted her in his life. Marriage was the next step, one he'd pushed for since they'd left Dallas. His only second

thoughts were of how hard he'd pushed and if this were really her decision.

"You said you needed to think about what you wanted. You haven't had much alone time."

"I love you. It's the only thing I don't need to think about and that isn't going to change." She tipped her chin, leaning into him, her eyes closing before their lips connected.

When they were together he tried to make her forget everything else. Each kiss took him back to the beginning of their adventure. A curious kiss at an airport that had spoiled his chances of falling for anyone else.

"Let's get this shindig going. I hear the slots calling my name." George, playing the part of best man, rubbed his hands together.

"I still can't believe you invited this guy."

Lanning had kept them informed on the investigation and had kept their names out of the press—as promised.

"I wanted your aunt to be a part of things. So…" Jo slid her hands over his shoulders, smoothing his jacket. "You needed a best man if I had a best gal."

"I have plenty of friends who didn't play me like a fool." He winked at her proving he wasn't upset. He actually appreciated George. And Jo knew that.

"But *I* don't know them. At least not until we get back to Denver."

It was time. Their turn. The coordinator waved them inside the doors. Levi watched the woman he loved link arms with his aunt and march to the front of the Vegas wedding chapel. Everything was set and in a few minutes, Jo would be his for life.

"That's one great woman you've got there," George said, slapping him on the back. "Appreciate the invite."

"I never had the chance to thank you for loaning me

your truck or setting me back up with my girl." He handed his best man the wedding rings he'd bought without his fiancé's knowledge.

"Don't mention it." George shrugged off the thanks. No one had mentioned the help he'd given Levi during the search for Jo. Help that had contradicted the Bureau's orders.

"If you take your spot, George, we can get this party started," Jo said, returning with her chapel-provided bouquet.

George kissed her cheek and took his place next to the minister waiting with his aunt up front.

"You're very beautiful," Levi told Jo, suddenly wondering how he'd gotten so lucky.

"This is it, Marshal Cooper. Care to walk me down the aisle?"

"It would be my pleasure, soon-to-be Mrs. Cooper." He hooked his arm and patted her hand once it was in place. "Is that going to feel weird to you? Being Jolene Cooper?"

"It's the only name that's ever felt one hundred percent right."

\* \* \* \* \*

# COMING NEXT MONTH from Harlequin® Intrigue®

## AVAILABLE MARCH 5, 2013

### #1407 COVER ME
#### Joanna Wayne, Rita Herron and Mallory Kane
Three men sworn to uphold the law return home to New Orleans, seeking the women they loved and lost—and vengeance against the men who destroyed their lives.

### #1408 TACTICAL ADVANTAGE
*The Precinct: Task Force*
#### Julie Miller
Opposites attract as a streetwise detective and brainy scientist team up to save the KCPD crime lab from a killer out to destroy any evidence of his crimes.

### #1409 RUN, HIDE
*Brothers in Arms: Fully Engaged*
#### Carol Ericson
When carefree Jenna Hansen married navy SEAL Cade Stark on a whim, she had no idea she was signing up for a life on the run. Now she has to run for two.

### #1410 THE PRINCESS PREDICAMENT
*Royal Bodyguards*
#### Lisa Childs
Despite their night of passion, royal bodyguard Whit Howell believes all he can offer Princess Gabriella St. John is his protection; he doesn't know he's already given her a baby.

### #1411 STRANGER ON RAVEN'S RIDGE
#### Jenna Ryan
When Raven Blume seeks refuge at her ancestral home in Maine after a family trauma, she is horrified to find that a stranger has taken residence in her house...or is he really a stranger?

### #1412 DEADLY FORCE
*The Detectives*
#### Beverly Long
Claire Fontaine doesn't want Detective Sam Vernelli's protection—she wants something more. But can either of them forget their traumatic shared past?

You can find more information on upcoming Harlequin® titles, free excerpts and more at www.Harlequin.com.

HICNM0213

# REQUEST YOUR FREE BOOKS!
## 2 FREE NOVELS PLUS 2 FREE GIFTS!

## HARLEQUIN
# INTRIGUE

### BREATHTAKING ROMANTIC SUSPENSE

HI13

*Jenna Stark has been on the run for three years, but she'll do anything to protect her son. Even rely on the one man she thought she'd never see again....*

The doors squealed open and she stumbled down the steps. Looking both ways, she hopped into the street.

Gavin wailed, "I wanna snowboard."

She jogged to the sidewalk, glancing over her shoulder. Was the man by the truck looking her way?

What now? She hadn't gotten too far from her house… and Marti's dead body. She couldn't go back. She couldn't get her car—the mechanic just got the part this morning.

*Think, Jenna.*

She couldn't put any more lives in danger. She'd have to hop another bus and get to the main bus depot in Salt Lake City. She had cash…lots of cash. She could get them two tickets to anywhere.

Hitching Gavin higher on her hip, she strode down the snow-dusted street in the opposite direction of the truck— like a woman with purpose. Like a woman with confidence and not in fear for her life.

She turned the next corner, her mind clicking through the streets of Lovett Peak, searching her memory bank for the nearest bus stop.

"Where are we going, Mommy?"

"Someplace warm, honey bunny."

*Half a mile away, in front of the high school.* That bus could get them to Salt Lake.

She'd start over. Build a new life. Again.

She straightened her spine and marched through the residential streets on her way to the local high school.

When the sound of a loud engine rumbled behind them,

her heartbeat quickened along with her steps as she glanced over her shoulder at an older-model blue car.

When the car slowed down, its engine growling like a predatory animal, she broke into a run.

She heard the door fly open and a man shouted, "Jenna, stop!"

She stumbled, nearly falling to her knees. She'd know that voice anywhere. It belonged to the man responsible for her life on the run.

Cade Stark.

Her husband.

*Don't miss the heart-stopping reunion between two people—a spy and a single mom—desperate to give their son a future.*

*Pick up Carol Ericson's*
*RUN, HIDE,*
*on sale in March 2013,*
*wherever Harlequin Intrigue® books are sold!*